OEDIPUS

THE BRANCHING ROAD

By the same author

Guide to Greece (with Michael Haag), 1978

Delphi and the Sacred Way, 1987

OEDIPUS

THE BRANCHING ROAD

NEVILLE SPENCER LEWIS

FOR MY TWO SONS, DAVID AND KASPERI

ISBN: 9781527269873

Cover design by Colin Elgie

Mapping: Dominic Beddow / magneticnorth.net
Elements of mapping © OpenStreetMap contributors

Pausanias, *Description of Greece*, Book 10.5.3-4, translated by the author:

Proceeding from here [the Phocicon, the assembly place of the Phocians] you will come to a road called the Branching Road [Σχιστή οδός, Schist Road]. On this road Oedipus killed his father. Fate caused memorials of the sufferings of Oedipus to be left throughout Greece. As soon as he was born, they pierced his ankles and left him exposed on Mount Cithairon in the territory of Plataia. He was brought up in Corinth and the area of the Isthmus. Then the land of Phocis and the Schist Road suffered the pollution of the murder of his father. Thebes is even better known for the marriage of Oedipus and the wrongful act of Eteocles. The Branching Road and the rashness of Oedipus upon it were the start of his troubles, and the tombs of Laius and the servant who accompanied him are still in the very middle of the place where the three roads meet, and above them stones have been gathered and piled up. According to what people say, it was Damasistratus, the king of Plataia, who found the bodies lying there and buried them.

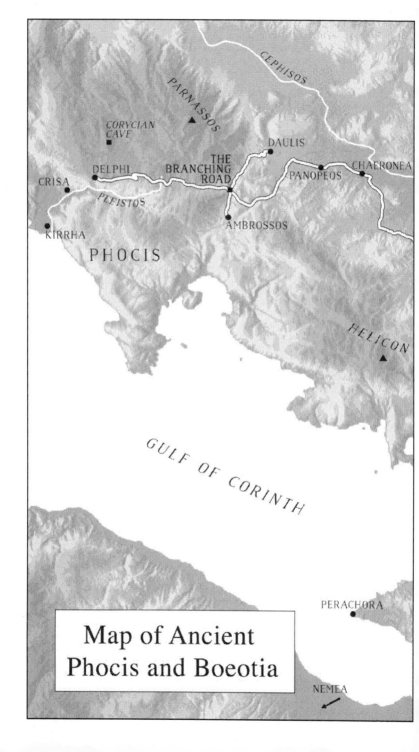

CEPHISOS

PARNASSOS

CORYCIAN CAVE

DAULIS

DELPHI

THE BRANCHING ROAD

CHAERONEA

PANOPEOS

CRISA

PLEISTOS

AMBROSSOS

KIRRHA

PHOCIS

HELICON

GULF OF CORINTH

PERACHORA

Map of Ancient Phocis and Boeotia

NEMEA

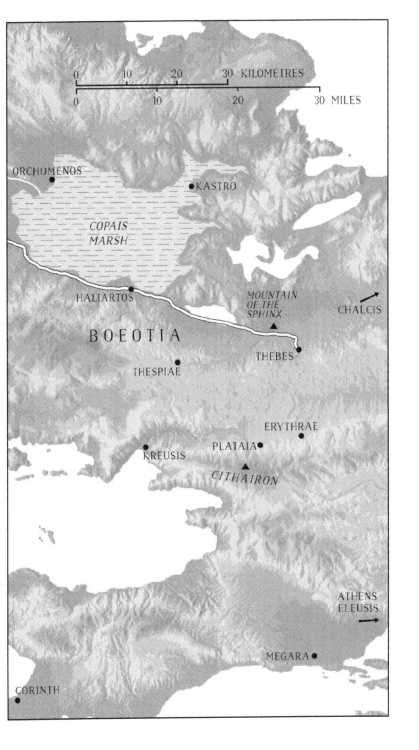

AUTHOR'S NOTE

According to myth, when Oedipus encountered Laius in Phocis the young man was seeking to escape the prophesy he had received at the oracle at Delphi that he would kill his father and marry his mother. His adoptive parents, Polybus and Merope, were the king and queen of Corinth. Believing these to be his true parents, Oedipus, having heard the prophecy, turned his back on the Corinthian Gulf and left Delphi in the direction of Thebes so as to avoid the oracle's outcome.

On his way he met Laius, king of Thebes, at the Branching Road, the junction of the roads between Delphi, Daulis (modern Davlia) and Thebes. At the crossroads there was an altercation between the two men who were travelling in opposite directions. Laius insulted and belittled the younger man, not of course knowing that this was his own son, and in the ensuing fight Laius was killed by Oedipus, who was equally ignorant of their true relationship. Sophocles describes the dire consequences in his play, in which Oedipus then succeeds Laius as king of Thebes and unwittingly marries his own mother, the widowed Queen Jocaste (or Jocasta).

So the traditional myth proceeds on the basis that Oedipus did not know he had killed his father. But what if he did? And how would he know this?

He had gone to Delphi because he was uncertain of his true parentage, or, at least, it had been challenged. He wanted to discover the truth.

What if Delphi had told him that he was not truly from Corinth but from Thebes and that his real parents had exposed him on a mountain to die at birth and he was in fact the son of the king of Thebes? He is therefore travelling to Thebes to claim his position as the heir to Laius. At the crossroads he meets Laius, who is travelling to Delphi to discover how to rid his country of the Sphinx. This is then a different encounter to the traditional version. On being told the man is Laius, Oedipus realises that according to the Delphic oracle this is his true father. There is an argument between the two men and when Laius strikes out at Oedipus, the young man is overwhelmed by fury with the man who attempted to kill him – his own son – as a child. A fight breaks out in which Laius is killed.

In this new scenario Oedipus travels on to Thebes knowing that he has murdered his father. Not revealing his role in the death of his father he claims lineage from the king. Laius' wife Jocaste is then overjoyed to learn that Oedipus is indeed her child. There is no incest with his mother, since both Oedipus and Jocaste are aware of their true relationship.

It is not, then, a story about marriage between mother and son; it is perhaps more concerned with the perennial rivalry between fathers and sons, the decline of the former and replacement by the latter.

In this version, Oedipus has a secret which he knows – that it was he that killed his father – and he has to endure the guilt of this. In the original myth the tragedy of Oedipus is that he drives on the discovery of the truth until it is evident for all to see – hence the significance of his striking out his eyes since he had been betrayed by the world he saw and thought he knew. Not so now. He wants to hide the truth. Yet years later it is Oedipus' own son Eteocles who begins to investigate the disappearance of Laius and Eteocles' suspicions are turned towards his father...

*

What follows therefore is a variation on the traditional myth of Oedipus, telling the story on the basis that he did indeed know he had killed his father King Laius and as a consequence there was no question of his marrying the woman he knew to be his mother. The reader can judge whether such an approach has any merit.

*

There is the familiar lack of uniformity in transliteration of Greek words. I have also variously described the fateful crossroads where Oedipus met Laius as the Schist Road (Schist being straight transliteration from the Greek word) or the Branching Road (a rough translation). And for the curious, the stones gathered over the tombs in the middle of the crossroads remain to this day at the bottom of the Zemeno.

CHAPTER 1

Oedipus had always limped. His feet ached, particularly in the cold weather which sometimes afflicted even the land of Corinth. The palace was high up on the hill overlooking the fields and the sea, and often in winter the snow would come down from the north on a bitter wind and would cover everything below, loading the olive trees and weighing the branches to the ground. The snow would go, but the same icy wind blew through the gaps in the wooden shutters, raced along the draughty corridors in the old building and no amount of swaddling of his small feet by his mother or his nurse would help. He grew up with pain in his feet and often they were swollen.

'Swell-foot' was the name he was given by the other children even though Oedipus was the son of the man who ruled the city. Children are no respecters of rank, and they teased the boy with his clumsy feet when they ran about playing football or went down to the sea to swim. He did not altogether mind the name since it was given to him without malice and it excused his slowness in running and competing in some of their games; he also saw the nickname as a badge of acceptance by the boys who, though the children of the wealthier families in the city, were not of the royal family. And in any event, just as Swell-foot was slow in some of their activities, he compensated for this by developing his strength in the rest of his body, which meant that the others never dared to belittle him with any further physical slight. Oedipus grew up with a large chest and muscular arms that could instantly wrestle any of his friends to the ground. And he could swim further and faster than them all when in the hot summer days they spent time at the beach below the city.

As he grew up, the boy's looks were another thing which marked him out. Many years before, his father had wed a dark Assyrian woman of wide brown eyes and black hair, a great beauty whom he had met on an expedition he had undertaken east of the Great

Sea. She was exotic, yet her symmetrical features softened her strangeness and made her homely and familiar. Oedipus was also dark with regular features and brown eyes, and no one was surprised at his good looks with such a striking mother, even though by now she was much older. Apart from his position as the heir to the throne in Corinth, he had no difficulty in attracting the interest of the girls in the city. And Oedipus took full advantage.

Yet, behind this easy young life, as the boy grew older there was a shadow. At first only slight, later more defined. He was an only child and unlike all his friends he had no brothers or sisters with whom to play when his companions were not free. When he asked his mother Merope why that was, she was evasive and talked of the great difficulty she had had in producing him. Oedipus seldom spoke alone with his father, King Polybus, who was usually busy in the marketplace arranging affairs and deciding disputes, but one day when he did ask him why he had no brothers or sisters he received a gruff reply telling him that he was fortunate not to have any rivals to the throne. His father was, anyway, a man of few words and Oedipus was not inclined to press the matter further.

For a time the issue seemed less pressing. He accepted his role as the sole possible successor to the throne. Polybus was older than many of the fathers of his friends, and he could see that it might not be long before he succeeded him as king. He gave himself to the military training arranged for him and to such education as he required, which principally entailed struggling with the new alphabet. There was also a vogue for learning stories of the Great War at Troy and reciting them, but he had no aptitude for this and although he liked to hear about the leaders such as Agamemnon and Odysseus he found it difficult to remember the poems line after line since they were not yet written down. He preferred outdoor pursuits. He could ride a horse well and he enjoyed hunting, especially for the wild boar that lived in the hills around Nemea. His father was on good terms with the ruler of that region and the story had it that both royal families were descendants of Heracles, who had carried out his first labour by killing the famous Nemean lion. An early and treasured memory of Oedipus was when he had gone with his father to watch him hunt together with a kinsman from Nemea. As a little boy on this expedition he had even imagined they were hunting for lion, but instead he witnessed the strength and speed of his father in bringing down a large hog that came out of a thicket and charged straight at them. Polybus had evaded the charge and struck the boar in its flank with his spear and felled it.

*

It was on an occasion years after that event when Oedipus was seventeen and was approaching adulthood that he began to question the family story that he had been a late arrival for an otherwise childless couple. He and two of his close friends, Eudemus and Alexander, had asked the old king if they could go off for a few days to hunt boar. Polybus was too old now for hunting and was happy to see his son do as he did when he was still fit and strong. It was June and the weather was warm enough to sleep out. Oedipus was allowed to take one of his father's chariots. He and Eudemus travelled in the chariot behind two fine horses, and Alexander accompanied them on horse with two servants riding along with them as well. They had basic provisions – cheese and olives and bread. They would find good water in the hills behind Nemea and roast the meat they killed. A servant would be sent into the city to buy some of the dark Nemean wine which was prized for its quality. They had spears for the hunt, with fine iron tips, and short swords for any closer work.

After leaving the chariot and the horses with the servants at the point of the track closest to their destination, the three friends walked up into the hills and made camp in a wooded area by a stream that Oedipus knew well from previous hunting forays. A spring came out, cold, from under a large rock and flowed through the trees, a mixture of planes and oaks, and the dead leaves underfoot made a soft base for their fleeces. There they slept after a simple meal. The next day they planned bigger fare after the hunt. The servants were to return with the wine in the afternoon after stabling the horses and the chariot in the city.

And so it was to be, but it was marred by one – or rather two – significant events. In the morning they set off for the very place where Oedipus had seen his father kill the hog so many years before. He knew it well, as he had frequently returned there. It was a thicket, more a grove, of oaks which had grown mature over time and produced the acorns so favoured by the hogs. The plan as they approached the area and had located any boar feeding under the trees was for Eudemus to circle round the other side of the clump and by beating the trees with a club drive the animals out towards Oedipus and Alexander who would be waiting with their spears. It should have been simple enough to deal with one or more of the boar in that way, spearing any animal that came running out and avoiding the dangerous tusks in the process. But this day it did not go according to plan.

There was certainly a number of wild boar amongst the trees. They were making plenty of noise as they rootled around seeking out the rich acorns, and Eudemus was able to get into position on the far side without disturbing them whilst the other two stationed themselves some paces apart to tackle those that emerged, each armed with a stout spear. Eudemus then started to beat the trees and to shout, creating a noise sufficient to disturb the entire wood. Shortly after, a large hog came charging out of the trees and headed straight for Alexander. The idea was that in such an event Alexander would stand his ground and hope to spear the beast before it was upon him, whilst Oedipus who was standing a little to one side would spring into action, run the short distance towards his friend and thrust the spear into its flank. Stuck by two spears the boar would be sufficiently disabled for one of the men to use his sword to cut its neck.

But this was a larger than average boar with particularly fearsome tusks, and it was quick. It was upon Alexander before Oedipus could take more than a couple of steps. Alexander struck a poor blow with his spear and one of the tusks plunged into his leg before Oedipus was able to engage the animal with his weapon. The hog screeched as the iron tip bore into its flank and Oedipus forced the weapon further and further into the hog's innards until it finally subsided to the ground. It took but a moment for Oedipus to cut its throat with his sharp sword. But the damage was done, and his friend's thigh was streaming blood from the wound.

Alexander lay on the ground cursing his luck, whilst Eudemus who had rushed back around having heard the commotion found some cloth in one of their bags to bind around the wound. There was now a practical problem to get both Alexander and the dead hog back to their camp. This they did in two stages. First Oedipus and Eudemus supported their friend between them as they walked back down to the stream. Fortunately the two servants had arrived by then and one of them who was skilled in the task washed and dressed the wound as best he could, though he lacked the herbal remedy which was normally applied. Eudemus and the servants returned to retrieve the boar. It all took time and it was late in the afternoon, after the hog had been partially butchered, before a fire had been made and pieces of the meat began to cook.

As he was in pain Alexander decided to have some of the wine to improve his mood, unusually before the food was ready. Even though he mixed the black liquid with water from the stream, he had had several glasses before the meal was ready. He was sometimes prone to drinking more wine than his friends and this time he had every reason to do so. As his mood lightened, his speech became heavier.

At one point when they lay back sated with the rich meat the young man started. 'Oedipus my friend,' he said, 'you are not the hunter I have heard your father was.'

Oedipus sat up, at this point more amused than disturbed.

'Why do you say that? I despatched the beast quickly enough when he was upon you,' he responded.

Alexander pressed on. 'Yes, but you were slow to move when the boar came charging out of the wood. It is those feet of yours, Swell-foot; they slow you down.'

It was some time since anyone had used that name of him. And Oedipus, who had himself drunk plenty of the Nemean wine by this time, flushed with anger. He did not like being accused of failing to protect his friend owing to his bad feet. And, like any son, he also did not like being compared unfavourably with his father, even though he acknowledged that Polybus had a reputation as a skilful and bold hunter in his younger days. He nevertheless controlled himself and sat there silently brooding.

But Alexander was not done. 'Maybe you are not your father's son after all,' he said. The statement hung in the still evening air, like the smoke from the fire.

At this Oedipus stood up and stared at his friend, before speaking in as measured a tone as he could: 'What do you mean by that? Do you simply mean I am not as good a hunter as him, or are you saying something more?'

At this point Eudemus intervened and told Alexander to stop. But the young man blundered on as the wine caught his tongue.

'Have you never heard people say that your parents could have no children and that they got you as a foundling and brought you up as their own?'

Oedipus was dumbfounded. He had never heard this suggested before and had himself never questioned his position, even though he realised Polybus and Merope were old as parents and there had been the continuing mystery of his lack of siblings. He could not believe it was possible, particularly as this was the first time it had come to his ears.

Though he had learnt to be stoical by nature, for example in the manner he put up with the pain in his feet with resignation and no complaint, he could easily be roused to anger, a trait which was not to help him in the trials to come. He turned on Alexander and would have fallen upon him with his fists if Eudemus had not sprung up between them and held Oedipus off their friend who was lying on the ground with no ability to defend himself.

'Eudemus, what do you know of this?' Oedipus shouted.

Eudemus did everything he could to calm, indeed mollify, his friend. He asked him to sit down again by the fire.

'Oedipus,' he said, 'I have only once heard a rumour, nothing more, much as Alexander said. It was many years ago, when I was still a child. I remember my father talking to a shepherd who had come into the city to sell some animals. For some reason the man was asking about the family of King Polybus, and when he was told there was just the one son, he said he had heard that as an infant the boy had been found by a shepherd on Mount Cithairon having been exposed there with his feet nailed and bound up.

'The child had been brought back to Corinth and there adopted by the king and queen because they had no children of their own. I remember my father dismissed this talk at the time, and I gave it little further thought. Maybe Alexander can say more – but perhaps it is best that nothing more be said.'

Undeterred, Oedipus turned again to Alexander. 'What then have you heard?'

Alexander could probably have continued, but realising the trouble he had caused replied briefly that he had heard rather less than Eudemus. All he added was that he hoped the scar caused by the wound proved as helpful to him in future life as that on Odysseus' leg in the story when, on his return to Ithaca, Odysseus' nurse had recognised him from the scar on his leg caused by a boar's tusk when he was young.

The evening ended on a sour note. They had indeed killed a large fat hog and feasted upon it, but Alexander had a nasty wound and Oedipus for the first time, but not the last, was deeply troubled. As he lay there with the crackling of the dying fire his mind ruminated on what had been said. Could it be true? It would make sense of many things – the advanced age of his parents, his lack of siblings and the problems with his feet. He certainly had something to discuss on his return to Corinth with those he had always believed to be his parents.

CHAPTER 2

Merope was in her room when Oedipus returned to the palace at Corinth. He had always adored his mother just as she had doted on her only child. He could remember as a small child sitting on her lap in front of the fire as she told him how she had grown up in Nineveh, then a relatively small city on the banks of the river Tigris. He would play with her long dark hair as she told how she went with her mother and sisters to wash their clothes and swim in the clear water and how she watched her father and uncles astride their chariots as they set off on a lion hunt. She spoke with a strange accent and as he grew older the boy would tease his mother about how she pronounced the Greek words. For him, familiar as he was with her, and warm and soft as she was when he nestled against her, his mother always retained something a little mysterious, like the scent carried on a foreign wind. And she often enhanced the mystery by speaking strangely, elliptically, elaborating her stories in such a way that Oedipus was left uncertain as to what she truly meant.

And so it was on this occasion when Oedipus raised the question of his parentage. He was shy to do so, diffident even, since he hated the idea that he might hurt his mother in any way by entering into discussion of such a difficult issue. He did not know how best to begin. He thought he would start by telling her about Alexander's accident and how his friend had blamed him for being too slow to come to help when he was attacked by the boar. She was sitting in front of a mirror combing her hair which was now flecked with greying strands. He stood behind her and told her about what had occurred at the hunt.

Then he went on. 'Mother, I have often wondered how it came about that my feet are so clumsy, why they ache and how I grew up to run so slowly. Did I have an accident when I was very young, before I can even remember?'

Merope was surprised to hear Oedipus ask this again now that he was almost an adult. He had frequently talked about his feet when he was a child, and his mother had simply reassured him that there was nothing wrong with them truly and that when he grew up they would be different. Now that he was almost a man and nothing had changed that approach no longer seemed realistic. Merope had dreaded her son asking questions about his feet when he was older as she feared it could very easily lead to the truth emerging about his being a foundling.

She prevaricated. 'Well, you remember how your feet used to swell up and ache and so you were late at walking and you did not enjoy running when you were little.'

She then went on to tell a long story about one of her brothers who had trodden on a big thorn when he was little and how this had made for a bad wound which the Assyrian doctors had taken a long time to cure and in fact had to enlist the help of the priests in the temple. This account was becoming increasingly long and elaborate in his mother's way, and Oedipus tried to cut her off.

'But did I have an accident, or did something strange happen to my feet, like their being bound up together for some reason?' he asked.

Merope could not think of any good reason why a child's feet might be bound up in infancy that she could give as some credible explanation to Oedipus, and she was certainly not willing to tell Oedipus the truth without the agreement of her husband, Polybus. She knew the reluctance of Polybus to tell Oedipus the true circumstances. He would not want his son to have his world crash about him with that discovery or to question his feelings for his adoptive parents with all the uncertainty as to his true parentage. Again Merope did not really address the question.

She finally said, rather vaguely, 'I don't think you had any accident but you just seem to have had slightly misshapen feet.'

Oedipus was tempted to put to her exactly what Alexander had said and ask her if it were true. But out of deep love for his mother he steered away from it and said no more.

Part of the young man wanted to forget the question. It would be easy to return to his normal routine, and continue his training for the city games, where he hoped to gain a prize in wrestling. But the thought would not go away – he wondered whether he really was the child of Polybus and Merope. In the warm nights of summer he lay awake, brooding. Finally he decided he must speak to Polybus.

However by the time Oedipus spoke to his father, Merope had long since told Polybus of her conversation with their son. She had decided for herself that Oedipus should know the truth. She was a follower of the goddess Astarte, whose cult she had brought from Assyria and who was worshipped for her fertility and sexuality. Merope had shown her devotion to Astarte as a younger woman but was not then blessed with children of her own. As a result she had always felt an inadequacy in the presence of the goddess and moreover did not enjoy the deceit that the apparent birth of Oepidus involved. It had been difficult enough deceiving the populace of Corinth that she had borne a child, but she doubted she had escaped the far-seeing eyes of the goddess. She wanted the position put right. And she felt that Oedipus was old enough and strong enough to know the truth. After all, there was no need for this to be made known more widely, and it could still be kept secret within the immediate family, even if Merope also bared her soul to Astarte.

Polybus would have none of it. His concern was less the mental welfare of his wife or the reaction of his son. More importantly for the king, if this became known as he feared it would sooner or later, he would be left without a true heir to the throne of Corinth, and that could only play into the hands of his possible rivals. There were already mutterings about kingship and whether there should evolve a more collective form of leadership in Corinth, and the lack of an heir to the throne would only increase such talk. He told Merope that they were to deny any suggestion that Oedipus had been adopted.

So when Oedipus raised it with his father one day as they were going down to the fields to inspect the crops which were now ripening under the summer sun, Polybus dismissed not only the suggestion that Oedipus' feet had been bound when he was an infant but then exploded at the idea that he had been adopted as a foundling and was not the king's true son. He was so angry at this point that when Polybus demanded to know where this rumour had come from, Oedipus found an excuse to ride off since he feared for the safety of Alexander if his name was mentioned.

The result of his conversations with his parents left Oepidus no wiser. Certainly his father's extreme reaction surprised him. The young man dwelt on it for several days until he felt there was only one solution, to consult the oracle at Delphi across the water of the Gulf to the north-west of Corinth. From the roof of the palace in the upper part of the city, the great mountain of Parnassos had been pointed out to him many times, and he knew that Delphi lay on its slopes. Perhaps the priestess there could dispel any doubts as to his parentage.

His mother had often talked of the oracle, prompted in part by her long interest in Astarte. Merope knew of the association of Delphi in former years with the earth goddess, Gaia, and understood Astarte to be the child of Gaia. Although Astarte had no place at Delphi this connection with Gaia was enough for Merope to have taught her son the importance of the oracle. The irony was that by this time the priestess, the Pythia, was no longer thought of as the voice of the earth-goddess but of the new northern god Apollo who was said to have killed Gaia's snake, the Python, and had taken over the sanctuary for his worship. Oedipus knew little of the arrangements for consulting the oracle, but he was aware through his mother of its increasing prestige. He also knew that any consultation would have to be in the summer months, since it was said the great god went away in the winter and the Pythia then fell silent until the following year.

There was a practical problem for Oedipus. He had of course to wait until he had competed in the games, but this would be soon. More importantly he did not dare to inform his parents of the reasons he was travelling to Delphi. He had to find an excuse for going away, for leaving the region of Corinth for the first time in his life, having never been much further than Nemea. This took time for him to devise.

The city of Corinth was at this time one of the bigger trading ports in Greece. It had two harbours, one on the Gulf from where the ships sailed westwards to the new lands of Italy and Sicily, and the other on the Great Sea itself from where they could reach Athens and ultimately Egypt and the mysterious lands further east. There were riches to be had nearer home too. Since northern invaders had come down and destroyed the large city of Crisa, in whose land Delphi was situated, the large plain below it running down to the port of Kirrha was largely bare and uncultivated. Herds of wild horses now roamed this land and it was rumoured in Corinth that these animals could be rounded up without difficulty and brought back home over the sea. Oedipus concocted the plan that he would lead an expedition across to capture a number of the better specimens. Once over there, since they would be gone for some time, he could make his way up to Delphi and consult the oracle.

It was not difficult to persuade Polybus of the virtues of this idea, since Oedipus was now coming of age and the old king thought his son should indeed be proving himself in this kind of way. Merope was less happy. As a mother she was loath to see her boy depart for any prolonged absence, particularly as it was possible the expedition might meet resistance. Kirrha, although now only a relic of the large settlement it had once been as the companion town to Crisa, was still populated and those living there, Phocians they were known as, might not be happy to see foreigners taking the animals away, even if they appeared to have little use for them themselves. However Oedipus was determined on this course, and he had the support of the king.

Later in the summer the young prince set out across the Gulf with Alexander and Eudemus, each commanding a ship with a small complement of competent sailors, some of who were particularly skilled with horses. In fact it was no better than a raiding party as they had little idea how many horses they might capture and how many they would anyway be able to transport home. Polybus suspected that if it went well this might be the precursor to a more ambitious project. At the western port Oedipus embraced both his father and mother before he finally left, little realising the significance of that moment.

They spent a night beached on the southern coast of the Gulf across the water from Kirrha. The following day the ships were able to put up their small sails and be blown by a southerly breeze across the water towards the Crisaean plain. In the distance they could see above the tree line the outline of Parnassos. The great mountain lay like the reclining figure of the goddess Gaia herself with its peaks protruding either side of her girdle. Oedipus knew the oracle was below the steep cliffs that showed light grey in the bright sunlight between the coast and Parnassos, but he could make nothing out from the sea.

As they sailed, the ships were accompanied by a small pod of dolphins, which reminded Oedipus that according to one story Apollo himself had come to Delphi in the shape of a dolphin carrying his priests on its back. When finally they landed at Kirrha they pulled up the ships onto the sand outside the village and the men made camp. Whilst the others devised plans as to how in the days to come they were going to set about capturing the horses which they could see in the distance beyond the rudimentary houses,

Oedipus straightaway decided that the next morning he would set out on foot to go up to Delphi. He planned to arrive at Delphi that day, make any necessary arrangements for seeing the oracle the following day and return to his companions on the third. He had no idea of what would lie ahead and how his life would be completely changed.

The way to Delphi was through the plain beside the empty bed of the Pleistos river to the valley under the sanctuary and then up towards the cliffs of the Phaedriades where the small village lay close by the oracle itself. The former city of Crisa, which had sat astride a hilltop below Delphi and which had formerly ruled over the entire area including Delphi (which was still known by some as Crisa), was in ruins after being destroyed by the northern invaders some generations before. Oedipus was unsure of what sort of reception he might get from the impoverished souls who still lived amongst what remained of the place, and so he kept to the lower route. And the port of Kirrha was then sufficiently insignificant that there was no toll upon visitors going up to Delphi from the coast as was to be the case later.

Oedipus set off without anyone paying him attention. He carried a stout staff for the walk and he wore a belt with his small sword; over his back he had a cloth bag with a little food for the journey, some water, and most importantly pots with the new geometric designs that the potters were now making in Corinth and which he hoped to use in exchange for his lodging and his visit to the oracle.

It was hot that day, in the airless plain, although the track was easy enough as it slowly made its way towards the valley. Once there however Oedipus had to make his way up the side of the hill, which was certainly steep, and then up through the terraces that had been carved below the village of Delphi. Finally he arrived at the scattering of modest houses that formed the settlement. The young man had first to find somewhere to stay and he was directed to the house of one of Apollo's priests. There he could stay and also hope to arrange a visit to the Pythia. By this time, after walking for much of the day, his feet were aching and he was tired and hungry.

The oracle was yet to develop into the business of later days, visitors were still few and in these simple times little was required in the way of payment, the priests and above all the priestess herself believing that it was a solemn duty to obey the god Apollo in conveying his knowledge to those consulting him. Nor was there even a temple as such. Oedipus was surprised to learn that the Pythia was housed in a small building made largely out of boughs of laurel, cut out of the trees of bay laurel which were scattered over the slopes below the cliffs. This he could visit the next day following the gift to the priest of the most handsome of the pottery vessels he had brought from Corinth.

Oedipus had already made known to the priest the nature of the question which he wanted answered, having disclosed that he was supposedly the son of the king and queen of Corinth but that he remained unsure of his true parentage and had even been told he might be a foundling who had been exposed as a baby on Mount Cithairon. He needed to know who he really was, and if Polybus and Merope were not his father and mother, then who were? But the priest was evasive and suggested that the Pythia herself did not give such clear answers; although the great god Apollo was all-seeing, the responses had to be siphoned through the mouth of a mortal and, though the Pythia was Apollo's mouthpiece, human fallibility was such that the responses by the priestess needed interpretation.

The priest offered to provide this service at the cost of a further piece of pottery. He was an old man who had served Apollo for very many summers and whilst genuinely reverential knew how best to use his role to advantage. He said finally that when he took Oedipus to the Pythia in the morning he would help him frame a sensible question. After this Oedipus was at last given something to eat. He then fell asleep in a corner of the priest's simple dwelling.

The priest was old, almost as old as the Pythia. They had worked together for many more than the eighteen summers that represented the lifetime of the young man. They had experience of hundreds of consultants over the years. Something about the story told by Oedipus stirred the old man's memory. He recalled that years ago the king of Thebes had been a consultant of the oracle. King Laius and his wife had also been childless and the king had enquired of the oracle whether he would have a child. Laius had received the surprising answer that he would do so, but would die at its hands. That was what the priest remembered. And a traveller passing through Delphi a couple of years afterwards had added a surprising sequel. It was rumoured that Laius, despite his best efforts to avoid lying with his wife after the prophesy, had done so one night after a drunken banquet and a son was later born to Jocaste. After much argument between the royal couple, to Jocaste's dismay the boy was taken from her, given to a shepherd on Mount Cithairon and there exposed to die. The old priest became troubled recollecting all this and hurried away from his house that evening to speak to the Pythia.

At this time of year in summer, when she would give forth her responses, the old woman slept in a small hut next to the laurel temple where her tripod stood. The sun had long departed the cliffs of the Phraedriades above, and the Pythia was asleep. When roused, after rinsing her face with some of the water ducted into a nearby basin from the springs on Parnassos, she remembered King Laius and his question. It was not often that Delphi was consulted by a king and she confirmed that she too had heard the rumour about the child. The thought that arose was whether or not the young man who was presenting himself with confusion as to his parentage was in fact the very child who had been born to Laius and who in pursuit of the prophesy delivered by the Pythia had been exposed by his parents on Cithairon. Could that child have been found and later adopted by the king and queen of Corinth? So far as the old pair could judge, the timing was about right.

And they realised with horror the consequences of the earlier prophesy. If this consultant was truly the son of King Laius, Oedipus was still liable to kill his father, however this was to come about. That was all the more probable if Oedipus was now told that Laius was his father since he was likely to go to Thebes to seek out his real parents. The oracle could then be blamed for bringing about such an outcome. As the oracle sought to establish its reputation for veracity and retain its integrity free from any suggestion of being influenced in its responses by anything other than the god himself, both the priest and the Pythia could see no way out of the problem. The Pythia would have to repeat the words of Apollo whatever that might entail. But if the priest could help frame the question so as to allow some ambiguity in the response, they could hope that whatever occurred subsequently could not necessarily be blamed upon the oracle. Fortunately the priest also had a hand when it came to interpretation and perhaps that was another opportunity to put a gloss on the truth.

The next morning Oedipus cleansed himself in the Castalian spring where the water comes down from Parnassos at the junction of the two great grey cliffs, the Phraedriades. Then he walked up the hillside between the bay trees and the cypresses, accompanied by the priest. As they went, the priest discussed with Oedipus what he was going to ask the oracle. The old man was anxious for the young consultant simply to ask to whom he was to offer a libation of wine to honour his father, and persuaded him that in answering this the Pythia would reveal who the true father was. It was to be hoped that

Apollo would not be moved to repeat any prophesy that Oedipus would kill his father, and in any event the priest could wrap the response in a vaguely expressed and innocuous hexameter, as was his skill.

By the time the two men arrived, the Pythia was already in the House of Laurels and they passed through the entrance door to find that the old lady was sitting on the tripod near a small cleft in the rocks, chewing leaves of bay. The inside of the small building was filled with a vapour that was rising from the gap in the rocks next to her seat. It carried a sweet-smelling fragrance that appeared to be affecting the Pythia as she swayed gently with her eyes closed muttering words which Oedipus could not catch. Light filtered through under the eaves catching the strands of smoke rising up to a small hole in the roof. He stood there for some moments transfixed by what he saw and he wondered if the great god Apollo was truly going to answer his question through the mouth of this old woman sitting in a trance-like state on top of the bronze three-legged structure gently shaking a branch of bay in one of her hands as she moved slowly from side to side.

The young man stood respectfully a few paces in front of the Pythia with his hands crossed in front of him. The priest prompted him to ask his question of Apollo.

'To whom shall I pour my libation of wine in order to honour my father?' he asked quietly.

The Pythia swayed slightly faster causing her to shake the bay a little more loudly. She was still chewing the leaves, which made her eventual response more difficult to hear as bits of bay leaves spilled from her mouth as she spoke.

Oedipus could make little out from what the Pythia said in her apparent trance but he caught some of the words clearly enough. It seemed that she was directing him to pour a libation to the god Dionysos in the city of Thebes. He thought he heard the word 'king' at some point. He turned around and asked the priest if there would be more. The priest shook his head, and the two men left the presence of the Pythia, with Oedipus disappointed at the brevity of the reply. The priest was relieved: he realised that Apollo was pointing the way for Oedipus to identify his father as the king of Thebes; but that since Oedipus was being instructed to honour his father the earlier prophesy given to Laius that he was to die at the hands of his son might have been overtaken by the later one. Oedipus fortunately appeared to know nothing of this grim forecast anyway.

So what then does this really mean, Oedipus inevitably asked. Mention of Dionysos was no surprise, even apart from his association with wine. Not only did the god reputedly rule Delphi during the winter months when Apollo was away from the sanctuary but he was also the patron god of Thebes and so it would be natural to pay homage to Dionysos in that city. But what else was meant by this short answer? What of his father?

But the priest would not be hurried. He now had to translate the ravings of the Pythia as best he could into one or more short metric lines which would make some sense to the enquirer and preferably leave some ambiguity in case the apparent meaning might need to be reinterpreted. And so he arranged to meet Oedipus later in the day at the rock of the Sibyl to give him the oracle in its finished form. It turned out to be simple.

Oedipus stood in the shade of the large bay laurels near the rock in the late afternoon as the priest gave a simple answer, indeed an instruction.

'Worship Dionysos and honour the ruler of rich Thebes.'

He had his answer, yet what of his father?

The priest smiled. 'You cannot expect too much of the Pythia. Your question was how to honour your father. The answer is to honour the ruler of Thebes. Ask yourself then who that is.'

Oedipus had heard that Laius was the king of Thebes, and so he naturally answered 'King Laius'. The priest smiled again – Dionysos was the patron deity of Thebes and in that sense also its ruler, but he did not point out that neat ambiguity. The young man turned away, in the firm belief that his true father was indeed Laius. This was the man who must have caused him to be left on the mountain to die. Yet Oedipus was now being told to honour him. He left the sanctuary, no less troubled than before.

CHAPTER 3

Oedipus walked back to the priest's house. It was too late in the day to travel to Kirrha, and he was not expected to return until the next day anyway. He had much to ponder. He had started the day as the apparent heir to the king of Corinth, and now he had learnt that his real father was in fact the king of Thebes. Moreover he knew that King Laius had tried to kill him and, knowing nothing of the prophesy that the king had himself received, Oedipus could only think the worst of his father for such an act.

He sat that evening in the increasing dark of the simple house, lit only in patches by a small number of oil lamps, in the village of Delphi. The priest gave him wine to drink and a little meat. Oedipus sat on his own and thought. What was he to make of the two people whom until now he had always understood to be his mother and father, the warm and exotic Merope and stern but kindly Polybus, who had given him life after taking him as a foundling? Was he to turn his back on them now and go and claim his rightful position at Thebes? And how should he regard King Laius, the father who had abandoned him to die when he was a defenceless baby? How could he ever feel true kinship towards such a man?

Yet that man was his true father it seemed and it was from him, not Polybus, that he should inherit a throne. In his privileged position as the heir to one throne it did not seem at all surprising that he was truly the heir not to that throne but to another, but the consequences seemed immense. Was he simply to present himself at Thebes on the basis of a statement from the Pythia that he should honour the ruler of that land? How would he be greeted if he claimed to be the son of the king, when the child should have been long dead? Laius was unlikely to be welcoming to a child whom he had tried to kill and who now mysteriously reappeared claiming descent from him. The black wine, which was young and very strong, made Oedipus morose and ultimately sleepy, with no answers in sight to these questions. The best he could do was to sleep on it and hope that the gods, perhaps Apollo himself, would shed light on his problems by morning.

He rose the following day as the light came up and first touched the Phaedriades above the village. He should be returning to Kirrha and finding his companions with such horses as they had captured. But his head was heavy with the wine from the night before, and his mood had not lightened. His anger had not abated as he mulled over his father's actions. He could not just turn back to Kirrha and return to Corinth as if nothing had happened. He felt he had to confront his father, king or not, if only to see whether Laius would now accept him as his heir. After all, once the truth was out, he no longer had a strong claim to the throne of Corinth, however much his adoptive parents might wish it otherwise. His future lay in Thebes, even if the way ahead looked difficult. And so Oedipus obtained some things for the journey east. He found someone travelling from Delphi down to the coast whom he asked to find Alexander and Eudemus and tell them that he had been delayed and would return to Corinth his own way. With that he set out, again on foot, towards Thebes.

He kept high on the side of the mountain, skirting the edges of Parnassos as he walked east along a track which lay through holm-oaks and wild olives. Above him he could see eagles circling against the blue sky. Across the valley he could look over to Mount Cirphis where a path plainly zigzagged up its flank to some fields. On his side of the valley he had to get over the saddle which contained a huddle of rough dwellings where lived the shepherds who kept their sheep and goats up above on the open area below the fir-covered heights of the mountain. Here water fell plentifully down the hillside into large wooden troughs for the animals. As he paused to refresh himself, in the usual way that travellers are questioned he was asked by a friendly shepherd where he was going. Oedipus was guarded about this and deflected the question by enquiring about a mysterious cave which he heard lay high above this village, on a hillside facing the peaks of Parnassos, and which was dedicated to the great god Pan. The shepherd knew of it and had been up there; he even tried to interest the young man in ascending the mountain to visit it, but Oedipus had no interest in any such diversion, as it would have taken some time and he wanted to press on.

A little way beyond the small settlement the country opened out on his left and lay back against a row of huge limestone crags forming a continuous wall of rock. At the further end of this line a great cleft ran up into the rocks bringing the waters of the Pleistos down from Parnassos in winter before the torrent would then flow below into the valley on the right to take it towards the coast. The track had to negotiate the watershed, now dry, before entering an area of pleasant meadowland at the top of a long defile between the outliers of Parnassos and Cirphis. Here the way started to descend between two rugged hillsides. In places the stones had been collected to make shelters for the flocks of sheep that were guarded at different points by shepherds weathered by the sun. As he proceeded, dogs barked and then bounded towards him, forcing him to reach down and pick up small stones to throw at the animals to scare them off. He was used to this sort of attention from dogs at Corinth, but these dogs seemed bigger and more persistent. Fortunately the act of stooping down for the stones was usually enough to cause the dogs to withdraw. It was unnerving nevertheless and Oedipus remained on edge as he forced his tired feet along. He had never travelled before in this strange part of the country; he was alone except for the watchful and suspicious shepherds, and was unsure of what lay ahead. He knew however that he was bound to make this journey in order to fulfil the instruction of the oracle, and he must endure whatever the future held for him. His slow anger at the injustice which had been done to him by his father helped to drive him on.

The track was wide enough here for a chariot and horses beside the bed of the stream that in winter would have carried some of the water away from the higher levels of the mountains on either side. It was hot as he descended towards the base of the defile, and he was vexed and tired. Moreover whilst his route was obvious enough so far, he was unsure of the way to Thebes beyond this point. It was at the bottom of this descent between the two mountainsides that arose the true beginning of all his troubles.

Oedipus understood from his conversation with the shepherd in the last village that there were various roads at this point. There was one to Thebes and another track led to the city of Daulis; there was a third way, though he had not grasped where this was meant to go. The place was known as the Branching Road. He stopped just short of the crossroads, not sure which direction he should take. Over to his left there was a stone shelter where one of the flocks he had seen higher up would be driven for the night and where the shepherd at this time of year would himself sleep. But at this time in the afternoon it was still empty and there was no one in sight.

As he stood on the track looking about him, he heard the sound of chariot wheels and looked up to see a pair of grey horses pulling two men, one in a plain tunic grasping the reins and driving the animals, the other standing behind him holding a long spear. They were coming from the road directly ahead, which Oedipus presumed to be the direction of Thebes, though he was not certain. The chariot was going fast enough to throw up dust and he was reluctant to stand in its way, but he needed to know which of the roads was the right direction. He therefore remained where he was and stood there with his stout staff placed firmly on the ground.

The chariot came to a halt, the horses blowing and pacing the ground. The driver called down to Oedipus and asked what he wanted.

'I am travelling from Delphi and I would like to be sure of the way to Thebes. Is that from where you are coming?' the young man asked.

'Yes,' said the driver, 'and don't you know better than to stand on the road in the way of a chariot?'

Oedipus' temper began to rise. 'Are the people of Thebes so ill-mannered that they cannot assist a traveller on the road in customary fashion?'

'Don't you know whom you are addressing?' the uncouth driver responded. 'My master is none other than King Laius, the ruler of Thebes, and he has urgent business in Delphi. So step aside!'

Oedipus simply stood there, nonplussed. Was this really his father, King Laius? It was not how he imagined he would meet him. He had not foreseen confronting his father on a dusty road in the middle of the mountains in Phocis. He had envisaged a place more fitting for a prince to demand audience of a king and obtain an explanation about the circumstances of his birth and an acknowledgment of his position as heir to the throne. Instead any conversation now was going to be born of anger, and the upset and rage within Oedipus was only likely to be magnified.

And so it was. Oedipus stood his ground and turned to the regal-looking figure who had hitherto stood mute on the chariot. The man was wearing a red cloak of the finest thread.

'So, King Laius, you are so great that I must make way for you. Yet are you not the man who I have heard exposed his son at birth to die on Mount Cithairon?'

Laius was stunned by this accusation and at first said nothing.

'You answer not?' Oedipus railed at him.

Laius had believed his secret was safe and was astounded to hear reference to that terrible deed committed so many years ago.

'How dare you make such a dreadful accusation!' he shouted back. 'Why would I have done such a thing? Move out of my way!'

Oedipus did not move. 'Do you deny having a baby boy that you left to die amongst the wolves and jackals on a bare mountainside?'

Laius said nothing and turned his head away. Oedipus was beside himself with anger in the face of this denial.

'I am that son!' he finally hurled back.

At that instant the words of the prophesy given to Laius by the Pythia all those years before came back to him and he saw his imminent death at the hands of his own son who was here standing in front of him. In panic he ordered his servant to drive on. The horses started off and came at Oedipus, who only avoided being trampled by moving quickly to one side. As the young man moved, Laius lunged at him from the chariot with his spear and almost pierced his chest, but Oedipus was too quick and seized the shaft of the weapon and pulled hard on it. Laius fell from the chariot and landed at Oedipus' feet.

The older man tried to stand up.

As he was doing so Oedipus shouted again, 'I am the son you tried to kill as a child.'

'There was no such child!' said Laius in defiance, trying to seize his spear to continue his attack.

The chariot meanwhile had stopped a little further along the road and Oedipus could see that the servant was coming back down the road with a sword in his hand. He knew he now had to fight for his life. He felt only hatred for the man he understood to be his father, who having rejected him as a child refused to acknowledge him even now and had tried to run him through with his spear. He pulled out his short sword and as Laius went to pick up his spear from the ground Oedipus plunged the sword into his neck before turning around and despatching the servant, pushing his weapon deep into the man's bowels.

Both men were dead, their bodies lying in the road, their blood soaking into the dust. For a little time Oedipus sat on his haunches as the magnitude of what had occurred sunk into him. He had killed not only the king of Thebes but his own father. His anger still gripped him. Did not the man deserve to die for trying to kill his own son, not just once but twice – once when a baby and defenceless, and the second time now when he attacked him with a spear? What was he to do faced with the two armed men coming at him? At this point it was easy to justify his actions as the resentment at his father's cruelty towards him perfused his entire thinking. Only later would he pause to reflect further on his behaviour and would the doubts creep in.

Eventually his mind began to clear and Oedipus needed to decide what to do. The great birds which he had seen earlier in the day were now visible above, and he began to realise that these might not be eagles but vultures. It was against all rules of decency simply to leave the bodies of the two men for carrion, and so he dragged them both to the far side of the crossroads where there was a clear, level space. On top of them he piled enough of the rough and unhewn stones lying around as to create the appearance of a small natural mound, and there he left Laius and his servant. As for the horses and the chariot, he took them a short way down the road to the right which he later learnt led to the small city of Ambrossos; he spurred them on their way with a slap on their hind quarters and they disappeared from view.

Oedipus was again left with a choice. Where to go? Part of his purpose in travelling to Thebes, in order to confront his father, had already been fulfilled, albeit in a way which he had not sought. His first thought was that he should turn back and go home to Corinth, where his heart lay and where he had his kindly adoptive parents and friends. But the problem still stood that he no longer had any legitimate claim to the throne there.

On the other hand he had a genuine claim to the throne at Thebes, particularly now that his father was dead. And what of his natural mother? He stood and pondered all this for some time, having moved a little along the track to the left of the crossroads.

His instinct had been to step aside from the road to Thebes to distance himself from the events that had just occurred. The place where he was standing was a clearer route than the third direction at the crossroads along which he had despatched the chariot, and he suspected he was now on the road to the city of Daulis. He knew of that place and had heard of a ruler there called Tereus; he had understood there to be some bond of friendship with the rulers of Corinth. He therefore thought that he would travel there in the first place and rely on the hospitality of Tereus before travelling on to Thebes. He would not speak of the deadly encounter at the Branching Road, though he would probably have to give some explanation for his journey.

As if to help him decide, at this moment a huge black cloud had gathered above the crossroads, there was a massive clap of thunder, followed almost immediately by lightning, and he was assailed by hailstones; these stopped, only for him to be lashed by heavy rain. The shelter, which he hoped that Daulis would afford, seemed then the obvious next step.

To reach Daulis, Oedipus needed to make his way along the flank of Parnassos. The road was easy enough, relatively level. Again there were flocks of sheep, with several shelters. At one such place he saw a woman with some small children, who must have been staying there with the shepherd in these warm days of summer. As he came closer to Daulis the sun had gone off the land. On his right a path lay beside cypress trees towards the substantial stone walls of the city which he could see circling the top of a hill in a fine position commanding the fields in the plain below. Houses spilled down the hillside, and he could hear water in the valley beneath as he made his way up to the gates in the wall. No one prevented his entry and he soon found his way to the large building on the higher part of the acropolis where he was told Tereus lived. The king ruled over much of Parnassos behind Daulis and over a good deal of the Boeotian land that stretched towards the ancient city of Orchomenos. And his palace reflected this wealth.

Oedipus was nervous about presenting himself to Tereus. The association between this king and the ruler of Corinth was tenuous – one meeting some years before, and Oedipus had even forgotten the story of this – and he had not thought of any good reason to be travelling to Daulis. He could not easily pretend that he was on some sort of trading mission as he had no goods with him nor even any pots left, and he was not sure what Daulis was meant to trade with a substantial marketplace like Corinth, which had its own sources of wheat and oil and other agricultural products closer to home. The young man had, however, learnt in his short life that if you are to tell a lie you should stick as close as possible to the truth, so that there is less that can be found to be untrue. So he decided to say that he was indeed on his way to Thebes on some business of King Polybus (which he need not relate) but that since Polybus had spoken so well of Tereus he had thought to visit him on his way. Oedipus did not dwell on the fact that the journey from Corinth to Thebes did not lie very obviously through Daulis. He would if necessary invent a reason to have visited Delphi first.

In fact all these concerns were baseless. Tereus was so preoccupied with his own affairs that whilst he was perfectly friendly to his visitor he expressed little interest in him or his plans. Having welcomed Oedipus with customary greetings and offered him dry clothes, he introduced him to his wife Procne, and then having shown him the extent of his palace, took him up to the palace terrace whilst it was still light. This stretched as far as the city walls overlooking the extensive plain.

'That is the way to Thebes,' he said pointing to the old city of Panopeos perched on a small spur of the line of hills framing the plain to the south-east. 'Beyond Panopeos you can see Orchomenos, but you need not go that far; you can pick up the bed of Cephisos which will take you down to the Great Marsh of Copais. You will need to go round that by Haliartos to reach Thebes.'

This was helpful to Oedipus, but clearly Tereus had something else in mind.

'That is the way I shall be taking shortly on my journey to Athens. You have met my wife Procne. She is the daughter of the king of Athens. She has a sister called Philomela who is even more beautiful than her. My wife is lonely here and I want to bring Philomela to Daulis to keep her sister company.

'I visited Athens recently and I was very impressed by the girl. She sings beautifully, whereas Procne can hardly sing at all – in fact she twitters like a swallow, whilst Philomela sings like a nightingale. I want my palace to echo with that beautiful sound.'

Oedipus found the enthusiasm of the king for the singing of the sister surprising, and he suspected it had more to do with the beauty of Philomela than her voice. Tereus seemed unaware of how his plan might look to others; he was so taken with his own importance that he felt his life deserved this adornment and that his true motives did not matter. At dinner it turned out that Procne was equally keen for her sister to keep her company and had no idea of what might lie ahead. Oedipus, for all his youth, feared the likely outcome, and in years to come he had reason to feel justified in his apprehension.

CHAPTER 4

The next morning Oedipus set out for Thebes, two days away. Before he left, Tereus gave him a warning.

'I have not had to endure what I am going to tell you, because in travelling to Athens I have avoided the direct route by the city of Thebes. We have often had bad relations with them, so I always go another way. But to travel into Thebes, you have to pass by the Mountain of the Sphinx, and I have heard stories of travellers falling foul of a beast that lives on the mountain. So far I understand not even King Laius has been able to solve the problem. You need to take care as you approach the city.'

The mention of Laius brought back to Oedipus the events of only yesterday. The king's servant had said they were travelling to Delphi, and Oedipus began to wonder what the nature of the enquiry was that took

Laius to Delphi. Perhaps it was precisely this question of the Sphinx. He saw the irony of the fact that, if Laius was on his way to obtain a solution to the problem at Delphi, now he himself had to undergo the test that the creature seemed to pose to anyone travelling to Thebes. He did not know how he was to deal with this peril and simply put it to the back of his mind for the moment.

Oedipus descended the flank of the hill on which the walls of Daulis stood and made for Panopeos across the fields. The city of Panopeos had once similarly lain on the hillside, but as he came close he could see its walls were ruinous. It had long lost its importance when it could send a contingent to Troy, and the few houses were now mostly huddled around the base of the slope beneath the former city. At one time it had guarded the direct route through the defile to the west which carried the road to Delphi; the way emerged at the Branching Road where it joined the higher route from Daulis. Now just a few farmers lived at the settlement, and he understood they were subject to the rule of Daulis, its more powerful neighbour.

The road passed by what remained of Panopeos and rather than make for the bed of the Cephisos in the centre of the valley Oedipus remained close to the line of the hills to the south. This would allow him to skirt the area of the Copais marsh which otherwise barred his route. The waters of the Cephisos here formed a shallow lake and although in the summer some of the water seeped away it remained a swamp and too treacherous to navigate for an unfamiliar traveller. Across the valley at this point Oedipus could see signs of the once great city of Orchomenos, which had previously controlled this entire basin and had drained the water so as to cultivate the land. But the city had then been humbled by the Thebans who had reputedly stopped up the sinkholes and caused the land to flood again. The Thebans liked to attribute this to Heracles. In any event it was safer for Oedipus to make his way along the side of Mount Helicon to Haliartos, itself perched on the top of a low hill raised above the fields at this point.

He obtained hospitality for the night in that small city whose chief virtue Oedipus found were the eels taken from the lake. There was more talk of the monster that lived on the mountain which now bore its name. Some described it as a woman with the body of a lion, others said it was a winged bird. Either way it was said that if a passer-by could not answer a riddle which the creature posed then the traveller would be devoured. The word Sphinx meant little to Oedipus, who was largely unaware of Egyptian beliefs. It sounded like a tall story to him and he was determined not to let this odd creature prevent him getting to Thebes.

When he continued the next day, he had left behind the lake. The road went through the middle of the Theban plain, with Helicon still lying to his right, now at a greater distance. The fields were busy with Thebans cultivating rows of corn. It was another warm day, and his feet were kicking up dust from the dirt track as he went. He needed to take frequent drinks from the water he had obtained from the spring at Haliartos. Then his eyes began to make out the unusual shape of a height ahead of him, to the left of the road. From the west the hill appeared stark and menacing, with something of the appearance of a monster; the upper part showed the outline of a woman's face whilst the lower part towards the road had the outstretched paws of a lion. Oedipus, even if he could credit the Pythia with supernatural power from her contact with the god Apollo, had a limit to his imagination. He could believe in heroes such as Heracles with his labours or in Achilles from the Trojan poems, but these remained mortals even if they had exceptional gifts and were not freaks or strange beings. He smiled as he understood, or thought he understood, the story of the monster. The beast was just a mountain, named after the mythical Sphinx due to its resemblance in shape – nothing more. Yet he did have one small nagging doubt – he wondered if a man like Tereus was likely to be frightened by a story based on the shape of a hill.

On he went approaching the so-called Mountain of the Sphinx, confident but a little wary nonetheless. Then as he drew level with the head of the Sphinx, an unearthly scream arose from a part of the supposed face in the hillside above him. He looked up, and there on a ledge where might have been the creature's mouth he could see swaying above him the unearthly figure of a hag with long black hair and dishevelled, filthy rags.

The thing was pointing down at him with an emaciated hand and she shouted out: 'You, where do you think you are going without paying your dues?'

Oedipus could not pretend that he was not scared by this mad apparition though he still believed that this was no mythical monster but something human, even if it was subhuman in its effect.

'What dues do I owe?' he shouted.

'You must give yourself to me,' came the reply, 'unless you can answer my riddle and only then can you proceed.'

Oedipus did not like to think what she meant by giving himself to her but instead asked her for the riddle.

'What is it that walks on four legs in the morning, on two at noon, and on three in the evening?'

He was fortunate – the answer came into his mind straightaway without thinking. 'Man', he said.

Having been given the correct answer, and being robbed of whatever forfeit she thought she could obtain from the traveller, the extraordinary creature let out an unearthly cry and threw herself to the ground in front of Oedipus, where she writhed for a time in agony and then expired. He looked down at her hideous face and, shuddering at the thought of what might have been his fate at her hands, he pressed on towards the city. He wondered if he could make use of his success in dealing with the so-called Sphinx when he arrived at the palace.

Here he was lucky. As he was making his way along the road he encountered a farmer coming in the opposite direction who asked Oedipus if he had seen the Sphinx and if so how he had managed to evade the creature. Oedipus told him what had occurred. The old farmer was overjoyed because he would otherwise have had to go a long way around to his fields in order to avoid the peril. He was so impressed by the young man's achievement that he said he would escort him to the palace where he would announce this triumph. As they walked together, the farmer confirmed that King Laius himself had set off for Delphi a few days before to ask the oracle how to rid the countryside of the Sphinx.

'What sort of king is Laius?' Oedipus decided to ask the old man.

'Hot-tempered and difficult,' was the reply, 'and sometimes unjust and high-handed with his subjects. They say too he is not always reverent to the gods, though he seems to like Dionysos well enough, especially with his wine-cup in hand. I have wondered whether the Sphinx was not sent to us by the gods to punish our city for his irreverence.'

Oedipus had still not fully processed the events at the Schist Road or entirely taken in that he had killed his own father, even if in self-defence, and the gnawing guilt which would afflict him at times in the future had not yet beset him. But he found this description of the king comforting. Whilst he did not like to think that his father was a harsh and unjust ruler, certainly his own brief experience had confirmed that Laius was arrogant and bad-tempered. Perhaps the inhabitants of Thebes would think they were well rid of him if he never came back. Oedipus began to imagine that he might become a far better ruler than his father.

*

The city of Cadmus was no longer the great centre that it had been at the time of King Agamemnon at Mycenae. The invaders from the north had put paid to that. But it retained its walls around the Cadmea, the acropolis, and these walls had seven gates, through one of which he was guided by the farmer to reach the area of the palace of Laius. He was hot after the day's travel from Haliartos along the dusty fields, but that was the least of his problems as he contemplated his position. He was the son and heir of the king, it seemed, but he was also his killer. He had the prospect of meeting his true mother at last, but he did not know how best to present himself and how to disguise what had occurred if he was now to claim the throne as his. His one piece of good fortune at this stage was that he had solved the riddle of the Sphinx and the farmer thought this was cause for celebration. That was at least a good start.

Fortunately he had a little time when he arrived at the palace. The farmer excitedly told the servants of the young man's victory over the Sphinx, but the king was of course not there to hear it (as Oedipus knew only too well) and Queen Jocaste was also away from the palace. He was told he must wait until that evening, when the queen would return. In the meantime he was put into a small room by the entrance to the palace and given food and fresh water as an honoured guest.

During these hours on his own Oedipus realised that in the first instance he had to feign ignorance of the death of Laius. Sooner or later unless his body was discovered at the Schist Road the palace would have to accept that the king was not going to return. The next question for him to resolve was when he might reveal himself as the queen's son. This would perhaps best be done in a few days' time when doubts were arising over Laius, and Jocaste might then be more susceptible to accepting the addition of a son in lieu of the loss of a husband. Meanwhile, whilst maintaining that he had business to discuss with the king and queen when they were both present, he could perhaps be allowed to stay in the palace enjoying the hospitality bestowed on him for having rid the country of the Sphinx.

Jocaste returned to the palace at dusk, as the sun was sinking behind Mount Cithairon to the west of the city. She had a retinue of servants with her and explained that she had been visiting one of her brothers, Menoecus, at Erythrae just below Cithairon. She also brought back with her a younger woman called Epicaste, her brother's daughter, who looked remarkably like her aunt, so much so that it would be easy to mistake them, there being only a few years difference in age. Oedipus introduced himself to the women and explained that he had business with both the queen and the king when the latter returned. However this was entirely overshadowed by the celebrity he had earned by conquering the Sphinx. He failed to understand why the old hag had caused such problems when he had solved the riddle so easily, thus provoking her demise, but he was not given to modesty and accepted the compliments showered on him and happily accepted the invitation to remain in the palace until the return of the king. This was made more easy by the obvious admiration paid to him by

Epicaste, who was as struck by the young man as he was by her beauty.

In all this excitement he paid relatively little attention to the woman whom he now knew to be his mother, Jocaste. She had none of the exoticism of Merope in Corinth. Certainly she was dark, her hair draped in ringlets onto her shoulders, but her looks were entirely Greek. She was tall and held herself erect with the bearing of a person used to being obeyed. What she appeared to lack was the warmth of Merope, and Oedipus wondered if this was due to her not having a child upon whom she had been able to lavish her love, as his adoptive mother had done with him. Her initial conversation with Oedipus was polite but distant, and he did not know how when confronted with his claim to be her son she would react. By contrast Epicaste was delightful and very easy company. And she was the person who became his companion over the next few days when Oedipus was still a mere guest and the palace waited for the return of its master.

The first morning after his arrival, when Oedipus had washed and bathed and put on the clean clothes with which he had been provided, he sought Epicaste's company to go with him to the Temple of Dionysos. He had not forgotten the oracle's instruction to worship Dionysos and to pour a libation of wine to the ruler of Thebes. But he was now disturbed. The cold reality of his father's death was beginning to hit him more and more, particularly as he stayed as a guest in the king's palace which he alone at this time knew would never see its master again. The previous night, after he had been led to one of the guest rooms by Jocaste he slept little. He had recurrent dreams, or rather nightmares, of the events at the Schist Road, and he woke with the image of his father crying out at the fatal blow. Oedipus lay in a pool of sweat, half-awake, hoping the picture would disappear, only to realise that the event had indeed happened. Perhaps he could have avoided lashing out, he reflected, yet Laius had attacked first. He then remembered his anger and all the bitterness at his rejection at birth that drove him as he pushed his sword home. The thoughts whirled around his mind, and he began to wonder if he would ever be free of these furies. The least he felt he should do was go to the temple and pour a libation to the shade of the ruler of Thebes. He hoped it might help lay his father's spirit to rest and ease his own mind.

Certainly he was distracted by his beautiful companion, Epicaste. She was tall and dark like her aunt, and that first morning she wore a long white dress with folds that hung lightly over her body, emphasizing her young breasts and slim waist. He had never seen such a woman in Corinth. She seemed to glide over the ground as she walked as if she was barely touching the surface beneath her. When she smiled it lit her face, and her brown eyes shone. At other times her eyes were full of tenderness as she looked at him. To the young man she seemed like a goddess.

Oedipus did not explain fully to Epicaste why he wanted to go to the Temple of Dionysos. As a visitor to Thebes it was unnecessary to justify paying his respects to the patron god of the city. He found some wine in the palace, and Epicaste led him to the temple which lay within the Cadmeia and no great distance away.

Outside, the smell of roasted meat hung in the air from a sacrifice just made. The temple was not a large building and it was dingy inside, lit only in places by oil lamps. A wooden representation of Dionysos stood in the innermost part.

Leaving Epicaste behind him, Oedipus approached the god and poured his offering of wine into a basin on the ground in front of the statue. After some conventional words of worship directed at the god he quietly spoke to the shade of his father.

'Father, you caused me to kill you and send you to the Underworld. You were a harsh man but when I succeed you I shall rule justly and the citizens of Thebes will remember me as a good king and not you. But I shall honour your shade by bringing offerings to the memory of the father I never had.'

That way he hoped he would have peace of mind. He then realised as he stood there that he was probably wearing some of his father's clothes and that it would only be a short time before he was indeed likely to be king in lieu of Laius. He turned round and joining Epicaste he walked out in the warm sunlight, enjoying the woman's company and putting to one side all the uncertainties of the coming days.

CHAPTER 5

It was now about a week since Laius had left Thebes to travel to the oracle and it was several days since the fatal encounter at the Schist Road. Oedipus was a familiar figure at the palace where he spent most of the daylight hours with Epicaste who continued to bedazzle him. They sat and talked and laughed. He told her of his life in Corinth as a prince without revealing his true lineage. She spoke of the simple life in her father's house at Erythrae and how she frequently went for walks on Cithairon with her mother and sisters. Oedipus kept silent for now about his own association with that mountain.

One day they took two horses from the stables of the palace and rode over to Thespiae, below Mount Helicon. It was the time of the festival of the Muses on the summit of the mountain. The Thespians had come back down from Helicon to the acropolis, and on this day they were dancing around the statue of Eros, their patron, which stood in the centre as an unworked piece of priapic stone. The dancers, both young men and women, were drinking unmixed wine from tables beside them, and the mood was wild. Epicaste and Oedipus stood watching, and soon they too had joined the dance, holding hands and laughing into each other's eyes. As finally they retired to one side of the circle of revolving figures, Epicaste joked with Oedipus that Heracles was said to have slept with all fifty daughters of King Thespius despite being preoccupied by hunting the lion of Cithairon. Oedipus laughed that he was content with one woman, and he needed no other. As the afternoon turned to evening they slipped away, walking down from the low acropolis through the houses and into the fields. There they kissed and lay together on the soft earth for the night. When they returned to Thebes the next morning, they had decided they were to marry.

It was not the time though to inform Jocaste or for that matter Epicaste's parents. Laius had still not returned from Delphi and Jocaste had become increasingly concerned. It was over a week and there was no word of the king.

She decided to send a servant to enquire after him. If the man travelled by horse, he should arrive in Delphi the following day. Oedipus, still loaded with the anxiety and uncertainty of his position, tried to avoid Jocaste. He found this easy to do owing to his preoccupation with Epicaste.

The messenger duly returned with news, such as it was, four days later. It was almost two weeks since Laius had left. The messenger had reached Delphi, where he heard that the king had never arrived and he had not consulted the oracle. There was no news at all of him there. The next day the man retraced his steps and quickly arrived at the settlement of shepherds high on the saddle on the flank of Parnassos. None of the shepherds he spoke to had seen the king or his chariot. As he descended the defile towards the Branching Road he stopped to speak to every shepherd he saw on the way.

The story was the same, and so it was until having passed the crossroads and taken the direct road back towards Thebes he stopped in the narrow valley which took the road towards Panopeos. There he was eating his scant provisions, some bread and olives and goat cheese, and drinking from a cold spring that emerged below a huge rock under plane trees, when he encountered a shepherd from Panopeos who could help a little. He kept his flocks in this area and had seen someone who was most probably the king in his chariot with another man driving, travelling fast in the direction of Delphi. He had merely waved, without any conversation. That seemed to be the last sighting of the chariot.

The servant had further conversations at Panopeos, where others had seen the same chariot passing. It seemed that the king had therefore disappeared on the road somewhere between the spring and then the defile above the Branching Road. The man stayed the night in the town and some of those to whom he spoke talked of brigands operating on the road to Delphi which occasionally attracted wealthy visitors travelling from the east to consult the oracle. And since Laius was plainly hurrying to Delphi and had no reason to go elsewhere at the

Branching Road, there was no obvious explanation for the disappearance of the king and his servant other than that they had been attacked by robbers, even though there remained no sign of either of them or even the chariot.

All this the servant related to Jocaste in the main hall of the palace in front of Oedipus and Epicaste. At the news the queen threw herself down onto the stone floor of the palace in deep distress.

'Where is Laius, what has become of my husband?' she screamed as she pulled her long hair over her face and wept into it. Epicaste tried to console her aunt by holding her, but to little effect as Jocaste kept repeating Laius' name.

Then as the implication of his death became clearer, she wailed: 'What will now become of me, a queen without her king? I shall be cast out by his enemies, with no son to defend me.' She finally struggled to her feet and cried out to the absent Laius: 'What did you do when you defiled all normal feelings and exposed our son upon Cithairon? He is not here to defend me and look after your house and rule in your place. I have nothing more to live for!'

She again collapsed to the ground, as Epicaste gently stroked her head.

At this dramatic moment Oedipus wisely hung back – it was not yet the time to reveal his true identity, but the hour was plainly coming.

Jocaste retired to her room and stayed there for the next two days. The whole palace remained in mourning, with servants in whispered conversations in corners and corridors. No one knew what was going to happen now. As word began to get out into the city, some of the noble families sent representatives to the palace to enquire about the position, but there was nobody who could tell them. Laius had no brothers and Jocaste's brother Menoecus remained in Erythrae not wishing to interfere. Then on the third day the queen emerged from her quarters dressed in black. She was calm, and Oedipus felt that this was the moment to have the conversation which he had once anticipated so greatly but which now he dreaded.

'Queen Jocaste,' he started, 'I have still not told you the business that brought me from Corinth to this great house. I had hoped to reveal this to both you and the king, but this I now cannot do and I must talk to you alone.'

Jocaste sighed and looked reflectively out of one the windows in the hall at the fields filled with sunlight outside, as if she was trying to conjure up the figure of her husband returning from his journey.

'No, I do not think you will be meeting the king,' she said. 'The time for his return has long since passed and the only news is bad news. He will not be coming, and I am alone and a widow with not even the body of my husband to bury.'

Oedipus tried not to think of the bloodied figure now buried under stones at the Branching Road. He must only think of what had occurred long ago and what was to happen in the future and not concern himself with events of the recent past.

'You know,' he continued, 'I have come from Corinth where I have been proud to call King Polybus and Queen Merope my parents throughout my eighteen years. They nurtured me and brought me up as their son and the successor to the king.'

'I know you to be of good lineage,' Jocaste replied, little realising as yet of what lineage she was speaking.

'However, more recently I had reason to doubt that lineage.' Oedipus paused before embarking on the story which had brought him to this point. 'I learnt that there were rumours in Corinth that I was not the child of the king and queen and that they had adopted me.'

Jocaste was not yet fully engaged with this account, being preoccupied with her own grief and difficulties.

She simply said quietly: 'It is indeed a terrible thing to be childless when you crave children. Your parents were fortunate.'

'Yes,' said Oedipus, 'but maybe it is not so easy for the child. It was a great shock for me to hear that perhaps Polybus and Merope were not my real parents.'

'What did you hear?' asked Jocaste, out of a degree of distracted curiosity.

'That I had been found on Mount Cithairon with my feet nailed and bound up. I had been exposed to die but I was discovered by a shepherd from Corinth who took me back to the city, where I was adopted.'

At this Jocaste suddenly began to take real interest in the story. First she asked Oedipus to repeat how old he was, and he told her again he was eighteen. Then she asked him to tell her once more what had happened to his feet as a baby.

Oedipus said: 'I never knew exactly what had been wrong with my feet because I was too young, but I know I was slow to learn to walk and I could never run very fast as I grew older. My feet would become swollen and I was known as 'Swell-foot'. They remain a little clumsy and they ache when I walk a long way. You can still see some scars where I believe my feet were nailed.'

Jocaste was now so affected by what Oedipus told her that she had to sit down on a bench.

She asked one of the servants for water. 'So what brought you to Thebes? You said you had business with my husband and myself.'

Here Oedipus came to the crucial connection. He told the queen that he had been troubled by the stories in Corinth and how he had tried to speak to his mother about it but that she would not permit any real discussion and was evasive. Polybus was no more helpful. And so he had decided to consult the oracle at Delphi. He explained that although the response was ambiguous it pointed him towards the ruler of Thebes as his true father. For that reason he had decided to travel to Thebes.

The queen was still unable to accept the implication that Oedipus was her abandoned child. Her emotions were too raw with grief at the loss of her husband to cope with the burden of feelings that this fresh realisation could involve.

'But how are we to know that the Pythia is correct and that the baby exposed on Cithairon belonged to King Laius… and myself,' she added hesitantly. 'As I was married to him at that time.'

Oedipus seized upon the possibility that the queen accepted the child might be hers; that a child of hers had indeed been exposed to die.

'Do you mean that you did have a child at that time that was taken to Cithairon?' he asked.

There was a long silence as Jocaste sat still, and then her chest began to heave with sobs that rent her body until she screamed, 'Yes, I had a baby boy that I had wanted so much, but he took it away from me and insisted on killing it!'

No one could have been unmoved by this outburst. By now Epicaste had come into the room, and she went and sat next to her aunt, who was still sobbing uncontrollably. As for Oedipus, for the first time he began to feel pity for the woman who he felt must indeed be his mother.

'Why? Why did Laius do such a thing?' he asked.

Jocaste could barely get her words out through her tears. 'When he went to ask the Pythia whether we might have children he was told that we would have a child but that the child would kill him. So he refused to lie with me. Except one night he was drunk at the festival of Dionysos and he forced himself upon me and gave me a child. When it was born I wanted to keep the boy but he took him away lest the child grow up to murder him.'

'What happened to the boy?' Oedipus asked.

'He later told me that he had nailed and bound his feet together and given him to a shepherd to leave on Mount Cithairon.'

For Oedipus this was sufficient proof. 'I must have been that boy and you must be my true mother,' he finally said. He still kept his distance from Jocaste who was being comforted by Epicaste.

Jocaste looked at him through her tears. The realisation that she was at last looking at her child again whom she had thought had died all those years ago was still too great for her to take in.

She clung to her previous uncertainties. 'What proof can you give me that you are my son?' she asked.

At this point Epicaste, who had up until now said nothing, intervened.

'Oedipus, don't you still have the scars on your feet where they were nailed together?'

Oedipus took off his heavy leather sandals and moved closer to his mother, so she could see the small round patches on the top of both of his feet, white now against the darker surrounding skin. Jocaste looked down and fell to the floor clutching at his feet and kissing them. At this point Oedipus could restrain himself no longer and held her head in his hands, slowly raising it until he could bend down and kiss her cheek. Now his tears flowed, and he kept repeating 'Mother, my mother!' Finally he lifted her up and sat down on the other side of the bench from Epicaste and clutched his mother's hands in his.

It was some time before any of the three spoke. It was Jocaste who still had most to assimilate. Oedipus was only getting confirmation of what he believed already. But Jocaste was having to accept that whilst she had lost a husband she had suddenly gained a son.

At last she spoke: 'Laius has gone. But you are here, my son, in his stead. We have a new king, which I feared was not to be. What a blessing the gods have given me!'

Oedipus was only too aware of the irony of this, that whilst he had now provided his mother with a son, it was he who had taken away her husband. He resolved that he was never going to reveal what occurred at the Schist Road. His father could lie quietly in peace, and he would rule in his place, if the gods granted it. He could not undo what had happened with his father, whom he still blamed for the tragic events at the crossroads. But one burden had been taken from him – the decision by Laius to expose him as a child was no longer incomprehensible, some act of random cruelty. Laius had been simply doing what he could to evade the prophesy, even if it was abominably harsh. And now Oedipus could also draw comfort from the fact that he was merely the instrument of the prophesy – he was thereby exonerated from blame, or so he could allow himself to think.

CHAPTER 6

Jocaste took no time to inform the city that whilst Laius was almost certainly dead she had recovered a son whom she expected to be accepted as the new king. This revelation of course came at a most opportune moment, and some felt too opportune. There was disquiet among the noble families that this unknown individual had suddenly appeared in the city and was claiming a right to the throne, and many were sceptical that he was truly the child of Laius and Jocaste.

A meeting of the nobles was called at the palace when Jocaste could justify her claims, as indeed could Oedipus. Before the meeting there was much talk in the city. Oedipus had on his side the praise due for despatching the Sphinx, and word had also got around that he had been brought up by the king and queen of Corinth which suggested a princely pedigree worthy perhaps of the throne of Thebes. However there was still the doubt as to whether he was truly the child that was said to have been abandoned. Perhaps he was just an impostor.

One of the nobles had the idea to trace the shepherd to whom the baby had been entrusted by Laius to leave it on Cithairon. Enquiries were made of all the shepherds known to have flocks on that mountain. It was thought essential to track the man down before any meeting was held. It was summer still and all the shepherds were with their animals high up on the mountain, where they remained at night. There was the additional complication that any shepherd to whom the baby had been entrusted, even if the man was still alive, might feel he would be blamed for the child's apparent survival. It took several days for Helicon to be searched and contact made with all the known shepherds. Eventually an old man was found who remembered being charged by Laius to leave the baby on the mountain. And this man when questioned felt more happy that the child had survived and might yet be the heir to the Theban throne than concerned at having disobeyed any orders.

When the meeting was finally called, in the presence of Oedipus and Jocaste, the shepherd came forward and was asked to say what had happened to the child when it was in his charge. He was clearly a kindly man who had brought up many children of his own, and he told his story.

'One day I was called to the palace and I spoke to King Laius. It was many years ago, late summer it was, though my animals were still up on the high pastures and had not been brought down to the plain for winter. He was agitated and asked me to undertake a heavy duty.

'He told me that there was a child born in the palace who could not be allowed to live owing to a prophesy given him by the priestess at Delphi. I did not hear what the prophesy was, but it must have been serious because I had to take the baby with me and expose it to die on the top of the mountain. I did not like doing this but the king bade me do it and in those days I respected King Laius, though later on I believe he became too harsh to us Thebans.'

At this point there was a murmur of assent from the audience around him, and he was bidden to continue.

'So I agreed to do as the king asked and he gave me a small bundle. I could see it contained a little boy and that his feet were bound and that there was blood on the cloth. It was a dreadful task. I straightaway set off up to my shelter where my wife was staying at that time too, and I told her what I was charged to do. She could not bear to see the infant treated in this way and wanted to keep the child herself. But I knew we could not. Sooner or later the king would find out and we would be in deep trouble.

'We decided that I would find a shepherd from the other side of the mountain and see if I could give the baby to him to take away. In those days Corinth had the run of much of the land on the south side of Cithairon and the next day I found a shepherd from there who accepted the child. Whether I did right or wrong you can choose, but I at least do not have the baby's blood on my hands. It would not have survived any time at all up there with the jackals and the wolves.'

No one amongst those listening was prepared to blame the old man for his actions. And now there seemed little scope for disputing that the child supposedly found on Cithairon by a shepherd from Corinth was the self-same boy abandoned by Laius. Oedipus stood up at this point and took the floor.

'I realise the shock that the loss of the king has been for Thebes. And on top of that you have now heard of my unexpected claim to the throne. But I came to this city following a prophesy at Delphi and you know too that I have been brought up a prince in Corinth.

'On my way here I solved the riddle of the Sphinx which had been troubling this land for several years. Jocaste is satisfied that I am her son, and all the enquiries confirm it. I am worthy to be your king in successor to my father Laius.'

His speech was plain and unadorned, and his manner authoritative without being arrogant. The assembly broadly nodded its approval for the young man whom his mother, Queen Jocaste, then ostentatiously embraced to demonstrate her complete support. The meeting ended with loud shouts of approbation: 'The king is dead. Long live the king!'

The position which looked so bleak for the queen only a matter of days before had been reversed, and Jocaste was secure with her son as king in lieu of her husband. If the truth be known, given the ill temper and harshness of the late king, she was not entirely unhappy at the exchange. As for Oedipus, all had been accomplished. The Delphic prophesies had been fulfilled and he was now in his rightful place. He could justify his killing of Laius as being part of the gods' purpose, and he was at ease with himself. He managed to bury in the depths of his mind any remaining doubts about his own behaviour in confronting his father at the Schist Road, and there he was content to leave them, forgotten and with no reason to be brought to the surface again.

*

Now he could turn his attention to his marriage to Epicaste. She had remained at the palace throughout these many days since Oedipus had arrived, partly to support her aunt and then out of her love for him. The first step was to go to Erythrae and speak to her father. The following morning after the assembly of the nobles which had confirmed Oedipus as king, the two young people set out.

Oedipus was able to take one of Laius' other chariots from the stables and he took the reins with Epicaste standing beside him. They sped through the fields which were high with corn. It would not be long before the wheat was cut and the winnowing began. As they approached the city of Erythrae, they could see fat oxen grazing in the fields, many of them belonging to Epicaste's father, Menoecus. The city had long been under the control of Thebes and it was unwalled. Menoecus lived in a modest house built of stone in the middle of the city, but he belonged to one of the wealthier families in Erythrae and owned a large amount of land. His position had until now been underpinned by his sister's status as queen of Thebes.

The visit of Oedipus to see Menoecus was not a mere formality. In accordance with custom he needed the permission of the bride's father to marry his daughter and it was for him to arrange the marriage with the father-in-law. Oedipus also wanted to ensure that as an outsider who had suddenly ascended to the throne of Thebes he could not be criticised for riding over local sensibilities.

When they arrived at the house in Erythrae, it turned out that Menoecus could not have been more welcoming. News had come of the events in Thebes and he had heard of his daughter's attachment to the new king. The marriage of his daughter to Oedipus, her cousin, would secure his standing again, much as it had been secured previously by the marriage of Jocaste to Laius. He could see no sensible objection to the union. It was true that Oedipus was young to be married but Epicaste was older than usual, since there was a dearth of suitable young men, and Menoecus felt it was high time she started to have children. Any grandson of his would now be in line for the throne of Thebes.

The discussions between Menoecus and Oedipus were not therefore difficult. Subject to the matter of a dowry, the marriage would proceed and it would take place at the next full moon which was only in about ten days' time. Nor was the dowry itself a problem. Menoecus had ample numbers of cattle to provide this and he could afford to give Oedipus a portion of his herd together with some grazing land without seriously depleting his wealth.

All this was discussed and sealed with a handshake before a substantial meal of roast ox which Menoecus had ordered the household to prepare when Oedipus and Epicaste had arrived. Menoecus was a bluff, rugged farmer, of short stature and with a mighty chest. He had a ready smile and soon warmed to the youthful suitor who was of similar build to himself although of darker complexion, with hair the same hue as Epicaste. The father delighted in the obvious happiness of his daughter. Even if she would shortly be leaving his house to live in the palace at Thebes, this was close at hand, and the dynastic advantage outweighed any qualms of that kind. When the meat was placed on the table in front of Oedipus, Menoecus called for wine and the two men ate while the women including Epicaste and her mother waited upon them. Oedipus was compelled to tell the story of the Sphinx yet again. Later someone produced a pipe and a drum, and first the women and finally the men got up to dance, circling the yard where they had been eating. Epicaste then went off to sleep in her own room and Oedipus fell asleep at the table as the drama and suspense of the last many days finally took its toll.

The next day Oedipus felt he was in a fog at first, with the raw wine still befuddling him. Then, as the sun rose higher, it seemed more like a mist that enveloped him; he was light-headed, his mind swimming with the happiness that he would soon be with Epicaste as his wife. Later that morning he had to say goodbye to her until he would see her for the wedding. He would return to Thebes whilst she stayed at home with her family preparing for her marriage.

On the way to Thebes Oedipus rode out of Erythrae with Menoecus so that he could be shown the cattle and the land which he was being given as Epicaste's dowry. Some of the cattle were the oxen that he had seen beside the road as they had approached the city yesterday. Menoecus pointed to several fields on the level ground that were included in the dowry and he then indicated the higher slopes above where there was more land better suited for sheep.

Oedipus found it difficult to grasp just how much his life had changed in the last short while. He had left Corinth as a prince but had now become a king in another realm of great wealth; he had much land and many animals, and was soon to marry a beautiful wife. He was dazzled by his good fortune.

It was on his way back to Thebes, travelling by himself, when Oedipus realised that he had something that he must do before his marriage. Many weeks had passed since he had left Corinth and last seen his adoptive parents Polybus and Merope. They would not know what had become of him and would have no idea that his future now lay in another city where he had become king. There was just enough time for him to travel to Corinth before the marriage to see the old couple and explain all that had happened. But first he would need to be sure that his position in Thebes was safe in his absence. As he returned to the palace he was in a thoughtful mood with these fresh questions to ponder.

For almost the first time he had an opportunity to be alone with his mother Jocaste. She was still adjusting to the new regime, in which she was no longer the wife of a king but was now the mother of one. She was still mistress of her house but soon would also be yielding that role to her niece. When Oedipus greeted her on his return from Erythrae the queen seemed to have shrunk in stature and become old. For the first time he felt something akin to love for his mother, something beyond pity. She had been betrayed by life, her child taken from her and now her husband too, however difficult he may have been in recent times. The reunion with her son was some compensation but it coincided with her loss of power to another woman. Oedipus saw her as frail and when he first greeted her he readily put his arms around her and held her to him.

He explained to her all that had happened at Erythrae and told her of the dowry and the arrangements for the wedding. Then he told her of his plan to go first to Corinth to see his adoptive parents and revealed his fears about leaving Thebes at this sensitive time so shortly after becoming king.

Jocaste had a suggestion to make: 'Why don't you approach Antipoenus, who is the most prominent among the nobles and who gave you his support at the meeting when you were confirmed as king? If he says he will look after your position when you travel to Corinth, it will be safe for you to travel.'

Oedipus hoped that his mother might be an important ally in the years ahead, someone he could turn to for advice. He immediately agreed to this plan, and in the evening of the same day went to the house of Antipoenus which was a little lower down from the palace. The noble was not there but was in the marketplace where he and many of the other men of the city gathered in the evenings to converse and conduct their business. Oedipus took one of the older servants with him to lend him a little more status. He found Antipoenus easily enough and the two men went off to one side. The older man was pleased to be approached in this way. He had liked Oedipus at first sight and admired his directness. Antipoenus had no ambitions for kingship himself and preferred to leave management of affairs to others, provided his views were consulted and not disregarded. He enjoyed a quiet authority amongst his peers, and it would be unlikely that anyone would take serious action without his agreement. He assured Oedipus that he would look after affairs in the next week when the new king was away. With that assurance Oedipus felt free to go to Corinth.

In fact he spent the following day with his mother, as he wanted to cement his relationship with her. It was still very strange and they remained nervous with each other. She talked of her life with Laius and he spoke of his childhood in Corinth with Polybus and Merope. He wondered if he would ever feel at home anywhere – he no longer belonged in Corinth now that he had discovered his roots in Thebes and, so far as Thebes was concerned, he had not grown up there and he even felt uncertain with his own mother. He hoped that somehow his union with Epicaste would provide him a secure base where he could belong.

CHAPTER 7

The journey from Thebes to Corinth was not straightforward. He could either go past Erythrae over Cithairon towards Eleusis and along the coast via Megara, a long distance by land, or take the road down to Kreusis on the Gulf and hope to find a boat over to Corinth. Owing to the shortage of time, Oedipus thought the second route was too risky in case there was no boat to take him across the Gulf and that it was better to spend perhaps three days travelling overland but be sure of getting there in good time. He could more easily get a ship back from Corinth to Kreusis since Polybus could arrange it.

Again he took a servant with him, and the journey overland by horse was uneventful. With some reluctance he skirted Erythrae where Epicaste remained with her family and with less reluctance passed by Eleusis on the other side of the mountains. He knew of the Eleusinian Mysteries which celebrated the goddess Demeter and her daughter Persephone whose annual return from Hades brought spring and growth and fertility back to earth. That was all very well, he thought, but he lived in a newer world where the male gods like Apollo now ruled. For him the time of the overwhelming importance of any earth goddess was over, and he had no interest in the fanciful notions he had heard that the initiates in the Mysteries entertained involving an afterlife of sorts. He accepted that the dead enjoyed a bat-like existence such as he had heard in the recitations of the Trojan stories and expected no better for himself.

The road along the coast of the Great Sea from Eleusis looked across the water to the island of Salamis and went on to the city of Megara and then Corinth. It was an easy enough journey at this time. Previously the robber Sciron was said to have had his lair at one point on the rocks by the sea and to have terrorised travellers. Theseus was reputed to have killed Sciron as part of his labours. Oedipus wondered if in years to come he would be remembered as having defeated the Sphinx in the same way. The country was full of these stories, and Oedipus did not believe most of them, though he was inclined to believe the extraordinary feats of Heracles, who was after all a Theban of sorts.

As he rode along by the sea, he mused about the gods. He could believe in Apollo well enough. He had benefited from the god's far-sightedness through the prophesy which Apollo had given him via the medium of his priestess, the Pythia. He was also happy to pay lip service to Dionysos and Aphrodite and several of the Olympian deities, though he could not take them that seriously when according to the Homeric poems they had chosen opposite sides in the Trojan wars and they carried on their sexual relationships with even more abandon than humans. He did wonder why if they were so powerful no one ever seemed to come across them except in stories. Still, he agreed that it was necessary to make sure that you did not offend them and you paid them their dues in sacrifice and libation. But it was the host of weird mythological figures like Sciron that he could not accept. To his mind these were really humans whose powers had been exaggerated in the telling, assuming they existed at all. For Oedipus, true power lay in human agency through the medium of the sword and of just rule. He believed that his father, Laius, represented an older, harsher way of doing things, and the time had now come for a new breed of ruler, guided by principles of moderation and the avoidance of hubris or arrogance. He would not alienate the gods and he would do what was required of him, but for him man was to be the true measure of all things.

So he thought, as he approached Corinth on its high hill. His heart lifted as ahead of him he saw the familiar fields below the great walls of the city and then passed by one of the beaches where he and his friends had been swimming earlier in the summer, only a matter of weeks before his life changed totally. He looked forward in particular to meeting Alexander and Eudemus again. He longed to see his adoptive parents but knew it was going to be a difficult meeting. What solace could he give old Polybus and his dear mother Merope?

It was approaching dusk on the third day since leaving Thebes when he arrived at the palace. Several weeks had gone by since he had sent the message back from Delphi that he had been delayed there and was going to make his own way home. His parents would have been very worried by his absence, and his arrival home would at least be a source of rejoicing in itself. He wondered how he could use the happiness at his return to defray the news of his new alignment at Thebes. Not for long, he imagined.

Certainly when he entered the palace and saw Merope in her room she was overjoyed.

'We did not know what had happened to you!' she said through her tears. She told him that the expedition had returned from Kirrha with a number of horses and that they had got the message concerning his visit to Delphi and his delay there. She was spilling over with questions, as of course Oedipus expected, and before answering he thought she should send for Polybus, as he did not want to have to go through this a second time with the king.

And when the old man came, Oedipus told them. He told them the whole story except of course the encounter with Laius at the Branching Road.

The two listened at first mostly in silence. It came as no surprise that he had wanted to learn the truth about his birth, but they had no idea that they had been bringing up the child of the king and queen of Thebes. He recounted his victory over the Sphinx, how the city of Thebes was disturbed by the continuing absence of the king and how his true lineage was finally established. Then he went on to tell them about Epicaste and his imminent marriage.

It was at this point that Merope burst into tears. 'So you will live with your new wife in Thebes?' she asked.

'Of course he will,' intervened Polybus. 'He is to be king of Thebes and his new wife will be the queen, and we shall grow old here without our son. And even worse,' he went on, 'he will not be here to take the throne after I have gone. It is a disaster for our family.'

Polybus could not be mollified. He could see agitation starting among the nobles for some sort of collective leadership now that there was no heir to the throne.

'It is exactly as I said before to you, Merope. Once it becomes known that you are only our adopted son our position here is lost. That is why I told Merope to deny any such suggestion and why I denied it to you, Oedipus. Yet you went behind me and used the pretext of the expedition to catch a few horses at Kirrha in order to go to consult the Pythia. And see where we are now. Apollo's far-seeing knowledge is not always a help to us mortals.'

At this point Oedipus tried to divert the conversation, at least for a moment, and asked about the horse expedition and how successful it had been. Polybus was happy to talk about something different for a moment too and told Oedipus that it had been a great success – they had brought back as many horses as the ships would hold, and another expedition with more and larger ships was planned.

'We shall soon rival Megara in the market of horses,' the king said. 'It was a good initiative of yours, Oedipus... If only you had not wished for more when you went across the Gulf.'

Oedipus now had the germ of an idea. 'Father,' he said, as he certainly was not going to change the way he spoke to his erstwhile parents, 'Corinth is a sea-faring and trading city whilst Thebes is far from the sea, has no ships and will never found a colony across the seas waters as we have sometimes imagined we might do from this city. Thebes has the land, whilst Corinth has the sea. They are not obvious rivals. The two cities are not far apart, and they are the pre-eminent cities of central Greece. Under my rule in Thebes and with my strong links to Corinth they could become firm allies.'

Polybus was certainly struck by this concept, but still could not see a way through the problem presented by Oedipus no longer being his heir. Merope was happier than her husband at the good fortune of their adopted child, but saw little gain beyond that. The king added the gloomy observation that he could not even see how they could attend the wedding at Erythrae, since they could not absent themselves from Corinth as this critical time. It was no use pretending that the new situation was good for the old couple but Oedipus comforted himself with the thought that he was but fulfilling the dictates of fate and that he was not himself to blame for the turn of events.

After this difficult discussion, the young man decided he should seek out his friends Alexander and Eudemus and tell them his good fortune. He found them sitting together in the marketplace discussing the next step in the horse venture. When he arrived they both threw their arms around him. First, he listened to their account of the horses, but then they wanted to hear all that had happened to him. He told them everything, though again he left out the Schist Road. Only he knew what had happened there and he was going to tell no one. Whilst his parents in Corinth had been understandably upset by the news that he was now king in Thebes rather than the heir to the throne at home, Alexander and Eudemus saw it as a huge adventure for Oedipus and could also see the opportunities that might come to them in terms of visiting Thebes and trading with the city.

'Saffron,' said Eudemus, 'that is what I am interested in.' Oedipus knew little of the spice and its uses. Eudemus explained that it had important purposes in treating ailments, as an aphrodisiac and extensively for perfume.

'I have heard that in Phocis the crocus which produces the saffron grows up on the plain below the peaks of Parnassos near the Corycian Cave and that in Boeotia they make perfumes from it at Chaeronea.' Oedipus had passed through Chaeronea on his way south from Daulis to Thebes, though he did not stop; and on the road from Delphi he had heard tell of the Corycian Cave. These places were within a day or two's travel from Thebes.

'Well, when I have become established in Thebes, let us speak further about such a trade,' he ended.

It was time for Oedipus to go back to the palace for the night. He said goodbye to his two friends, but not before inviting them to the marriage at Erythrae in a few days' time. It was important that they came in the absence of his adoptive parents. He had no relatives to invite, and these two were his best friends.

He had one more day to spend at Corinth before leaving to return to Thebes. Polybus grudgingly agreed to arrange a ship to take him across to Kreusis the day after. He had some of his own clothes to take with him, and Merope was tearful as Oedipus set about gathering his things. Meanwhile Polybus had already begun discussions with some of the nobles about the future government of Corinth. Perhaps it would not end in disaster after all. Even so, he did not feel it was sensible to leave Corinth to travel to Thebes to attend the wedding.

The morning arrived for Oedipus to leave his adoptive home. There was no shortage of weeping from Merope especially, but the young man also had to cover his eyes to hide his tears. To mark this moment Polybus presented Oedipus with a magnificient white horse which had been captured on the Kirrha expedition and had just been broken in. Polybus also gave him a fine iron sword, newly made in one of the foundries in Corinth. Oedipus was only too happy to leave behind the weapon which had done for Laius.

*

Oedipus and his Theban servant set out the next morning at rosy-fingered dawn. The ship was manned by oarsmen and it carried a small sail to take advantage of the light breeze. They had to pass the city of Perachora standing on the tip of its peninsular pointing out into the calm waters of the Gulf. They could see clearly the new temple of Hera standing above the port, and then accompanied once more by dolphins they progressed swiftly to the harbour at Kreusis. Early in the afternoon they made landfall and the two men were able to reach Thebes on their horses when it was still light.

Jocaste was at the palace, where all the talk now was of the marriage in three days' time. Epicaste was still at Erythrae where she was spending time with her mother and her friends and relatives in preparation for the wedding. The full moon was three nights away and Oedipus and his entourage including Jocaste would travel over from Thebes early on the day for the ceremony and the wedding feast.

When the day arrived Oedipus took the largest chariot from the palace stables and instructed the grooms to hitch up the two finest horses for him to drive. Jocaste and her servants would travel behind in a wagon. The journey to Erythrae was along a relatively level track and although uncomfortable only took half the morning, and they arrived in good time for the ceremony at midday. First Oedipus went to the house of Epicaste's parents where he found the bride veiled amid a throng of family and friends. He was barely able to greet her amongst so much ferment.

Eventually the wedding party walked to the small temple of Aphrodite at the centre of the city. Epicaste's father had arranged for an ox to be slaughtered at the altar in front of the building. Some of the animal would be offered to the goddess, with the better parts taken back to the house and roasted for the wedding feast in the afternoon. Alexander and Eudemus were waiting outside the temple, having travelled over the Gulf the previous day. Oedipus introduced his friends to his bride, and the young couple then went into the temple together to offer the sacrifice in return for the blessing of the goddess. The priest sprinkled some water over the bride and groom. Following this purification the ceremony was done and the celebrations could begin.

The feast lasted all afternoon. The men ate first before the women were allowed to join them. When they did so, Epicaste purposively sat down next to Oedipus and at that moment she lifted her veil.

'Now I am yours,' she said to her young husband. Alexander and Eudemus who were sitting nearby marvelled at her beauty and gently teased the pair about the pleasures ahead of them. It was late in the day when it was time for Oedipus to take his bride back to the palace in Thebes. Once she was formally installed there, the marriage would be complete. The journey home from Erythrae was an excuse for a riotous procession of chariots, wagons, horses and pedestrians to make its way along a road accompanied by lamps, with drums and pipes piercing the evening air. When they finally arrived at the palace in Thebes Oedipus and Epicaste went inside and the gathering dissipated. The married couple went to their newly prepared bedroom and finally fell into each other's arms.

In the following days there was more feasting. Oedipus had his two boyhood friends to entertain before they returned to Corinth, and he was able to arrange a boar hunt on one of the days. This provided plenty of meat for the palace kitchens, and this time there was no incident when a member of the party was wounded. Epicaste began to assume control of the running of the palace, whilst Jocaste spent increasing amounts of time in her own rooms. The younger generation took over the dining table and Oedipus began to feel increasingly secure with the aid of Epicaste. So smoothly did she fit into the palace life that some of the servants would mistakenly call her Jocaste.

In time Alexander and Eudemus returned to Corinth, taking with them messages from Oedipus for Polybus and Merope.

As summer passed into autumn, with the corn all gathered in, the grapes picked and the olives beginning to fatten on the trees, Epicaste discovered she was pregnant.

Over the winter as the young queen bloomed, Jocaste faded and became more and more of a recluse, hardly stirring from her room. She was seldom seen and looked more like a wraith than a living soul; a paler version of her former self. Oedipus knew little of his mother's previous ways and with all the novelty of his position and his happiness with Epicaste he paid Jocaste little attention.

One evening Oedipus visited the former queen in her room. She was brushing her long dark hair while gazing wistfully into the mirror.

'I have lost my looks and become old. And, just as I have found a son to replace my husband and also gained a daughter, I shall be leaving you...' she said quietly.

Oedipus was shocked and asked what she meant. 'Where are you thinking of going?'

Jocaste turned away from the mirror and looked at her son: 'My time here is coming to an end. My mother, and her mother before her, both died at this age. I have no wish to stay longer. Although your father Laius was a difficult man and often treated me badly, I find it difficult to live without him. And just as you can take the king's place, so Epicaste can take mine. Many in the city even now mistake her for me as I once was. I am ready to go down to dark Hades.'

'Mother, how can you talk like this?' said Oedipus. 'You are still young and once your period of mourning is over you will regain your youthfulness.'

'No, I am done,' she responded. 'I do not resent my fate and the gods have so decreed it, but this is no longer my household to rule. I have nothing more to give here. When I die, please bury me with the normal obsequies. It will not be long, as I do not wish to live.'

There was nothing more to be said, and Oedipus left the room, hoping that this mood of his mother would pass.

In the following days as Epicaste came near her time to give birth, so Jocaste faded further, refusing all food and scarcely drinking any water. Finally as Epicaste went into labour and the women in the palace gathered around to help her, Jocaste breathed her last; her death eclipsed by the pandemonium surrounding the birth of a new child. He was called Eteocles.

The death of Jocaste could not have come at a more unfavourable time, since it was thought to be the worst kind of luck for the new child. Oedipus was simultaneously overjoyed with the safe birth of the boy and distraught by the death of his mother, particularly at this time. The only way he could think to deal with this dreadful situation was to send a message to Jocaste's brother, Menoecus, to take the dead woman for burial at the family tomb in Erythrae. So the day after Eteocles was born, the remains of Jocaste were taken quietly from the palace to Erythrae and there buried with a minimum of fuss. Few people in Thebes knew what had occurred to Jocaste. The new queen who looked so like her aunt ruled in her stead, and as time went on Jocaste and Epicaste become one in the popular mind. As the birth of one child followed another in the palace, some even thought that Oedipus had had unhealthy relations with his mother.

CHAPTER 8

The third year of Oedipus' rule in Thebes produced a second son, Polynices. He was born in the summer. A little later in the same year that the child arrived Oedipus had another visit from his two old friends from Corinth. They too were prospering. They had developed the horse trade in the three years since the initial expedition, and Corinthian ships were now frequently seen in Kirrha. They had travelled with their own two horses but had led several others to trade.

Eudemus wanted now to extend his interests into trading in saffron. He knew that the saffron crocus grew on Parnassos in the fields below the Corycian Cave and that the spice was obtained from the dried stigmas of the flower. He had spoken to traders in the port of Kirrha who had collected it from the gatherers themselves and taken it down to the sea. The problem they faced was that the ruinous city of Crisa below Delphi was host to numerous robbers who could prey on passing travellers and for whom the highly valuable spice was an obvious target. Eudemus speculated whether a better route from Parnassos might lie eastwards down via the Branching Road to the Boeotian plain where it could come within the control of Thebes. Traders from Corinth could ship the saffron from Kreusis, or Thebes itself could act as a centre for its distribution south to Athens or further eastwards and overseas.

The one unknown in this project was the city of Orchomenos, which lay to the north of the Copais marsh. The road which the traders would take from Parnassos towards Thebes skirted the territory of Orchomenos to the west. Thebes had humbled the old Mycenaean city in the distant past, but Oedipus knew that the new rulers at Orchomenos were looking for ways to exert their influence and restore the city's power. They might not want to overlook the opportunity presented by a lucrative spice trade passing along the edge of their land.

The first step was for Eudemus and Alexander to go up onto Parnassos and look at the crocus fields. The crop was understood to come in the autumn, and on the upland fields it would arrive a little later, about the time of the grape harvest in the plains and not long before snow sometimes came down from Parnassos.

The two young men had to hope that they had chosen the right time. Oedipus would have liked to join them but the young king was reluctant to leave the city for too long. Antipoenus remained an ally, but he was becoming old and Oedipus did not want to leave anything to chance. Epicaste now had two small children, Eteocles and Polynices, and though attended by a nurse she would find her husband's absence difficult. Besides, the king had his own fields to look after, both at Thebes and in the territory of Erythrae. So Eudemus and Alexander equipped themselves for a journey to Parnassos, and since it would be cold in the autumn nights on the mountain they took thick lambswool fleeces for their bedding. The plan was to be away for about two weeks. They also brought a couple of spare horses for barter in case they were successful in coming to an agreement with the producers of the saffron.

Oedipus himself made enquiries of the merchants in the city by going down to the marketplace where they usually gathered in the evenings. He seldom went into the city, since he believed a certain aloofness enhanced his authority, but equally he knew that he needed to be seen from time to time. Once again he sought out Antipoenus for his knowledge of the important traders. Together they embarked upon discussions to discover the possibilities of Thebes becoming involved in the saffron trade.

In fact there was no shortage of interest in the potential business but almost no experience of it. One merchant who had travelled as far as Crete had seen saffron being exchanged there but that was it. What all were agreed upon was that any trade route for its onward transport should not lie south over Cithairon. This was safe at the northern end through the position of Erythrae which was a close ally, but was less so at the south owing to possible interference by the cities of Megara and Eleusis. The best route would be either westwards to Kreusis or eastwards to the coast at Chalcis. From Chalcis Corinthian ships would distribute the spice further afield over the Great Sea. Oedipus could see the beginnings of an arrangement between the merchants of Thebes and Corinth that he had dreamt of in his conversation with King Polybus and which could indeed be profitable to both cities.

In the event, Eudemus and Alexander were gone for much longer than two weeks, and Oedipus was becoming concerned for their safety. Then towards the end of the fourth week they rode back to the palace in Thebes. They had indeed returned with some saffron and without the two spare horses. But they had a disturbing story to tell.

After they had taken refreshment they sat down with Oedipus and told him what had happened. The expedition had gone extremely well at first. They had ascended to the upland area below the Corycian Cave as they had planned and there they saw the vast beds of purple crocuses tended by local people from Delphi and other villagers from the lower slopes of Parnassos. The flowers were in mid harvest. The new blooms appearing at night needed to be harvested the following morning and the red stigmas removed for drying. The freshly picked stigmas when dried became the crimson threads constituting the spice.

The two visitors spent several days watching the process, sleeping out in the cool nights under the autumn stars. The crocus fields were largely under the control of a Delphian called Cleopompus, a short dark man who marshalled his workers with quiet authority. He was used to dealing with older traders who had struggled to these upland areas on elderly mules and was impressed by the two young men with their string of spirited horses hailing from the great city of Corinth, with talk of ships and overseas trade in the spice. Eudemus was able to strike a deal for the exchange of the two spare horses for several jars of saffron, and the groundwork was laid for a more substantial trade the following year with more of the animals and large quantities of Corinthian pots for storing and transporting the spice.

After about ten days the young men were ready to leave and set off down the mountain travelling back the same way they had gone up, in the south-easterly direction of the Schist Road. They had their two horses with several pots of the saffron spice slung about them. They described to Oedipus how they left Daulis to one side and passed by Panopeos and Chaeronea on down towards the Copais marsh.

It was then that the trouble arose. As they were approaching the small city of Haliartos, a group of half a dozen men rode up swiftly behind and surrounded them. They were armed with spears and swords. They demanded to know where Eudemus and Alexander were travelling and what they were carrying. The young men from Corinth, though outnumbered, declined to tell them, but it soon became clear that if they persisted in remaining silent the consequence would be a fight which they might well lose.

They played for time by asking where the men were from, and were told it was Orchomenos. The men pointed across the marsh to the north to the spur of Mount Chlomon at the base of which lay what remained of the Mycenaean city of the Minyans. They said the new ruler levied a tithe on goods passing through his land. Eudemus took the initiative and demanded that they were taken to see the new lord of Orchomenos; it seemed more prudent than merely to submit to a band of marauding horsemen who could take all their goods, particularly when they realised its value. At Orchomenos they might be treated as guests and be in a position to bargain their way out of difficulty.

And so it was, their story continued, that Oedipus' two friends found themselves as unwilling visitors to the home of the new ruler of Orchomenos. The old palace had been partially reconstructed after its destruction many years before, and the city was slowly renewing itself. The ruler was young, no more than thirty years old, and had pointedly given himself the historic name of Minyas. However on the first night of their arrival Minyas made himself studiously unavailable. The two visitors were put in the servants' quarters whilst their horses were taken away and stabled and they carefully guarded the jars of spice in the corner of the room where they were directed to sleep.

This went on for several days without any audience with Minyas. The men were free to wander around the old city, where they saw the great domed, circular tomb of the former kings, still decorated on the inside with bronze rosettes and with part of the ceiling covered with spirals and floral motifs. This had been no ordinary place and it must once have been a city of extraordinary wealth. The two young men from Corinth became concerned as to how the modern-day Minyas might be wishing to emulate his forbears and how their own enterprise might be at the whim of a man of such ambition.

It was noticeable how much rebuilding was being carried out in the city. At one point too as they walked around the outskirts of the built-up area they came across a group of men who were sitting in a circle on a flat piece of ground where one of them was drawing a map of the lake. The discussion was how best they could drain the waters once more so that the land could be brought back into cultivation. This would be news indeed for any Theban.

In the end Eudemus could see no way forward but to force the issue by demanding to see the ruler.

'Are we your prisoners,' he asked when he stood in front of Minyas, 'or are we your guests entitled to the normal laws of hospitality?'

Minyas replied: 'You are certainly not our prisoners but in accordance with our laws you must state what your business is when you cross our land and you must pay any taxes that we deem right. You have not done so!'

'But nor has anything been demanded of us as yet,' Eudemus calmly stated.

'That depends on what you are carrying,' said Minyas, 'and we still do not know.'

This had presented Eudemus with a dilemma – whether or not to reveal what they were carrying in the jars. The pots were not very large and it would be hard to pretend it was simply some normal agricultural produce like oil.

'Will you not settle simply for a tithe upon the number of jars?' Eudemus asked.

Minyas' answer was swift and inevitable. 'It depends entirely on what you are carrying.'

Since it would be only too easy for Minyas' men to check the jars, Eudemus felt he had little option but to finally tell him that they were transporting the spice saffron. Minyas knew little of the properties or value of this commodity but indicated he would consult with others before making his decision. He would give this the next day.

Eudemus explained to Ocdipus how he and Alexander then deliberated that night what to do, essentially contemplating whether they could perhaps escape. But the jars were numerous and would be awkward to carry on foot. And their horses were securely guarded. The best hope was that the Orchomenians would not grasp the true value of the spice.

The following day the two men had been summoned to go before Minyas to hear his decision. Minyas began by saying that he had spoken to some of the traders in the city, one of whom knew of the spice, its various uses and its true value.

'That trader even compared it to gold,' he said, 'yet you were attempting to smuggle it through our territory and refused to tell my men what it was.'

Eudemus had remonstrated with Minyas. 'By what law of god is it that says we must declare what we carry to anyone who enquires?'

Minyas had his reply ready. 'It is not the law of god, but the law of man – the man who rules the land through which you travel.'

'The law of the robber then?' interposed Alexander, becoming heated.

'No, the law of the stronger against the weaker,' Minyas continued.

And it was true that the two Corinthians were not in a strong bargaining position. Eudemus asked what the tithe was that it was proposed Minyas was going to impose on this consignment of spice.

The ruler answered at once: 'Half of the jars on this occasion because you failed to co-operate. In future if you declare the trade you will pay one-third.'

Eudemus shook with anger. 'Why then would we trouble to bring the spice through your land and not seek other routes if you impose such a heavy tax? Would it not be better to temper your demands to say one-tenth of the product? That way you may preserve both the trade and your tax. Otherwise you may receive nothing at all.

'Moreover we are on our way to Thebes as you know, where we are friends with King Oedipus. Do you want to incur his enmity by these actions? This city's rivalry with Thebes in the past did not end well for Orchomenos.'

Minyas saw the implicit threat in these remarks and bridled.

'Do not threaten me with such words, otherwise the normal rules of hospitality for guests in my palace may no longer be honoured. You now have a choice, to accept my decision and give up half of the spice and return home with the remainder and with your horses or to be cast out empty-handed. Reflect well, and consider that two-thirds of this trade passing through my land will still make a substantial profit for you.'

The two men explained to Oedipus that they felt they had no realistic alternative but to accept these terms, at least so that they could extract themselves from Orchomenos and return home with something, even if that was only half of what they had expected to bring. Oedipus listened to this account in almost total silence. He remained quiet for some time.

Finally he turned to the two men and said simply this to them: 'You have done well. The Minyans have overreached themselves. This could mean war.'

CHAPTER 9

There was a long history of rivalry and indeed warfare between Thebes and Orchomenos. In its great days before its destruction by the Northerners along with the other Mycenaean centres such as Thebes, Orchomenos had been strong and wealthy, as shown by the large royal tomb. It had managed to drain the basin to its south and cultivate the entire area until during one time of war with Thebes, their opponents had succeeded in blocking the sinkholes to the north-east and so flooded the plain again. It was reputedly the Theban hero Heracles who was responsible. And for hundreds of years since that time the Copais marsh had lain as a permanent reminder to the Orchomenians of what they had once been but were no longer. Oedipus concluded that the modern day Minyas wanted to restore Orchomenos to its former glory and power;

the interference with the trade through its territory and its extortionate taxation was a major step in that direction. But Oedipus also noted the ambition to drain the Copais lake. If that was to happen, then Orchomenos could indeed truly rival Thebes once more. For the king it was no longer just a matter of developing a secure route for the saffron trade – the Thebans had to keep Orchomenos in its rightful place as one of the lesser cities in Boeotia, unable to challenge the pre-eminence of Thebes.

There was nothing further for Eudemus and Alexander to do at this stage except return home to Corinth, where their connections might be of use if the position did descend into warfare with Orchomenos and Corinth might be persuaded to send men to side with the Thebans.

Meanwhile it was necessary for Oedipus to confront the Orchomenians. In the first instance he convened a meeting of the leading families in Thebes. Prominent amongst this group was Antipoenus. They all congregated in the hall of the palace.

Oedipus was the first to speak outlining the present state of affairs, in particular the level of taxation that Orchomenos was proposing for the future saffron trade when it passed through its territory. He could only assume that any other goods would be similarly charged. Oedipus saw this as a personal affront to his position as the ruler of Thebes and ended by suggesting they carried out a punitive raid on Orchomenos.

It was then the turn of Antipoenus to talk. As befitted his advancing years, he was much more cautious.

'I have long been worried by developments at Orchomenos, with its new young ruler,' he began. 'And of course I too am worried in case they can undo what our hero Heracles did in damming up the sinkholes and flooding the plain below the city. However once we do battle with them there is no knowing where it may end and what side the fickle gods may favour in the result. We must be slow to start hostilities. In the first instance I suggest we send envoys to discuss these matters further with Minyas. We may be able to find a solution to the problem.'

The meeting approved this moderate course since nothing would be lost by pursuing it. However Oedipus insisted that he should be a member of the party to visit Orchomenos. It was decided that in the first instance a herald would ride over to Orchomenos the following day to attempt to arrange a meeting at a later date between the party of Theban envoys and Minyas.

Antipoenus said he would send his son as the herald. 'The gods protect a herald, and I have no fears for his safety,' he added.

And so it worked out. The young man returned with an agreement that in a week's time Minyas would receive a party of Theban envoys to discuss the relations between their cities. Minyas simply specified that a maximum of ten men was sent. Who would be among the ten was the subject of much discussion. Antipoenus was reluctant to travel, and Oedipus preferred to leave him in control in Thebes. There was no difficulty filling the places of those who were to accompany Oedipus.

Before they left, Oedipus discussed with Antipoenus what they were trying to gain from the meeting with Minyas. The king was for demanding complete freedom from taxes on goods destined for the city, in particular on saffron. The older man asked, though, what they could offer Orchomenos in return. Oedipus said Thebes could agree not to interfere with the attempts by Minyas' men to free up the sinkholes and redrain the lake.

But, said Antipoenus, 'how else will they pay for such works unless they can tax the trade going through their land? I cannot see Minyas agreeing to waive all taxation – he needs the means for that project.'

They discussed the possibility that Orchomenos could in fact succeed in draining the marsh. Antipoenus thought that Heracles had done such a good job in blocking the drainage areas that it would be beyond the Orchomenians to achieve this in any event.

'If that is so,' Oedipus said, 'let us leave the question of drainage to another day. We won't threaten them there. We will simply threaten them with hostilities if they try to levy any taxes on our goods.' His elder pointed out that it was not uncommon for cities to exercise some levy on goods or even people passing through their lands, to which the king responded by saying that this depended upon the power of those being levied.

'Thebes will not be subject to such a levy,' he said simply. Antipoenus then left, expressing the fear that the meeting with Minyas was not going to be easy.

*

The ten envoys set out on horses for Orchomenos at the beginning of the following week. They took no arms or armour beyond their short swords. At their head rode Oedipus. They were hoping to return the following day. At Haliartos they were greeted by a small party of men from Orchomenos who rode with them along the shore of the lake round to the city. And unlike when Eudemus and Alexander were escorted into Orchomenos and taken to the palace, there was no delay before meeting with Minyas in the palace building.

Minyas, who was attended by several men, invited the envoys to sit in front of him and addressed Oedipus respectfully.

'Oedipus, son of Laius, king of Thebes, what do you mean to accomplish by coming here to talk with us?'

Oedipus reminded him of the history involving his friends Eudemus and Alexander.

'I am concerned', he said, 'that such an event does not recur.' He paused. 'Thebes is a great city with a past equally as illustrious as yours,' he remarked, hoping to gain by this unwarranted flattery. 'We would not expect trade passing through your territory, be it of saffron or more basic agricultural products, to be subject to a levy like you sought fit to impose.'

'It would not be unique for a city of the importance of Orchomenos to tax travellers in this way. I am told that the port of Kirrha is now charging visitors going up to Delphi from the sea,' Minyas responded.

'Minyas, perhaps it is a matter of choosing whom to charge and whom not to charge. Thebans and those trading with Thebes will not expect to pay such fees levied by your city. In particular those conducting the saffron trade will not accept such a penalty, since even a small part of the cargo if taken from them is of considerable value.'

Minyas countered: 'I accept that we were perhaps a little harsh when dealing with the matter previously. I proposed a continuing tax of one-third. If that is too much, I shall be content with a levy of one-tenth. This would be on all goods.'

Oedipus could see Minyas' position weakening and jumped on the concession.

'Minyas, I am glad to see that good sense is not in shorter supply in Orchomenos than elsewhere, but we shall not endure any tax upon the saffron trade. Other goods if necessary. You can have that, but not on the saffron.'

The young ruler of Orchomenos stiffened in his chair, as he gripped its arms. He was not used to anyone standing up to him in this way.

'Oedipus, we must differ for the moment. Let us leave this question to one side whilst you enjoy our hospitality. Let us feast together this evening, and we shall see where we stand tomorrow after a night's sleep'.

Certainly Minyas did his guests proud that evening, with plenty of roast lamb and kid from the uplands behind the city and young wine from the vines in the nearby fields. They sat around the large fire in the hall of the palace feasting until as the evening went on there was a recitation of some of the Trojan poems. Finally the men spread out on the floor on their fleeces and fell asleep. It was not clear how matters were to resolve the next day, and Oedipus remained concerned about what the morning might bring.

The break of the new day brought a chill in the autumnal air. The reality of the differences between the two sides remained. In further discussion neither Minyas nor Oedipus was prepared to compromise. Minyas stuck firm to his decision to impose a tax on the saffron passing through his territory, and Oedipus was adamant that he would not accept this being levied upon those trading with Thebes. Fortunately the time for the saffron to be brought away from Parnassos had passed for this year, and the problem could be postponed until the following autumn. The two rulers parted with friendly words but cold looks.

CHAPTER 10

The impasse over the levy proposed by Orchomenos was the first setback for Oedipus during his reign at Thebes. The position had not been concluded as he had wished, and he had even conceded the right of Orchomenos to tax some of the goods bound for Thebes. He found himself brooding on this over the winter, particularly as Minyas started to stop traders travelling through his territory and to take a portion of their goods. He realised he had committed a grave mistake making the concession without obtaining any safeguard from Minyas for the saffron.

The doubts about his abilities began to plague him. Was he truly fit to be the king of a throne to which he was entitled by birth but from which he was perhaps disqualified by the bloody means he had acquired it? He became anxious and began to sleep fitfully. His wife Epicaste realised Oedipus was troubled and sought to soothe him. Oedipus told her readily enough that he felt he had been outsmarted by Minyas and that he was concerned about what would happen the following year with the saffron. He did not confide his innermost fears since he could not reveal to her his latent guilt about the events at the Schist Road.

He began to visit the Temple of Dionysos more frequently in order to pour a libation in memory of Laius in the hope that it would satisfy his father's shade and bring him freedom from the furies which were starting to eat away at his peace of mind. The act of worship gave him an inner warmth, although it only had a limited effect and would dissipate later in the day. He wondered if he would ever be free of his guilt. On some days he felt better than others, when he was more able to rationalise and justify his actions. Not only could he tell himself he was justified in confronting his father who had abandoned and then disowned him before attempting to strike him with his spear at the fatal crossroads. In addition he could look to the unending process by which sons replaced their fathers in the management of affairs. It was a rightful sequence, part of the natural order. Yet it also implied that at some point in the future he might be a similar victim. That was a thought he could barely entertain now, with his two boys so young, but one day it would recur more strongly.

Life at the palace otherwise proceeded as you would expect, as one season followed another. In the early summer the following year, Eudemus paid a further visit to Oedipus to discuss the saffron trade in the autumn. Oedipus explained to him the course the negotiations had taken with Minyas and that he remained uncertain whether the traders would be able to proceed unmolested with their cargo to Thebes.

'I fear he will attempt to take his portion of the saffron in defiance of my position, Eudemus,' he said.

Eudemus was tempted to agree to the imposition.

'Would the loss of one-tenth of our produce be such a terrible result, when the remainder of the crop is so valuable?'

But Oedipus would have none of it. His status as ruler of Thebes was at stake. All those who had travelled with him to Orchomenos knew the position he had taken with Minyas, and if he was seen to have backed down this would damage his authority, possibly irrevocably.

'I cannot accept that, I am sorry Eudemus', he said. 'We shall have to provide protection to you when you travel up to Parnassos since you will be taking horses and pots for barter. And when you come back down with the spice we shall have to do the same again. There is no alternative, until Minyas yields.'

It was arranged that in the autumn the trading party from Corinth would come to Thebes with a string of horses and a consignment of pots and that Oedipus would arrange for them to be accompanied by a strong band of armed Thebans who would escort them through the territory of the Orchomenians probably as far as Daulis. Oedipus intended to visit Tereus once again and secure his help. It might be necessary for the Thebans to be quartered at Daulis to await the return of the men from Corinth with their spice.

So in midsummer Oedipus again set out northwards to visit King Tereus at Daulis. He took two of his servants and they rode over to the city where it lay dramatically on the outlier of Parnassos. They passed through the land of Orchomenos without problem. As they then travelled across the plain below Daulis, the Davliots were bringing in the first of the harvests of corn. It certainly looked peaceful enough. But the situation at the palace up on the acropolis was different. The atmosphere was dark, and Oedipus soon discovered why.

When Oedipus had last been there several years before, indeed the night of the events at the Schist Road, he had been welcomed by Tereus but the king of Daulis had been much concerned with the plan to bring his wife's sister Philomela to live there to keep Procne company, or so he said. Oedipus had been wise enough to suspect that the king's motives were not unrelated to the beauty of the younger sister. Now, when Oedipus presented himself again, Tereus was quick to confirm that Philomela had indeed come from Athens to live at the palace but was residing there as his wife.

He went on to explain that unfortunately Procne, his first wife, had fallen ill not long after Oedipus' previous visit and had sadly died. Pandion, the father of the sisters, when he heard of this, had kindly offered Philomela in lieu of Procne, and the ruler of Daulis had happily accepted this offer. Oedipus, as a guest, did not like to question this version of events, though given his host's obvious passion for Philomela at the time of his last visit the Theban wondered whether he was being told the truth. Certainly Philomela was beautiful enough, Oedipus noted, for Tereus to pursue, but at what true cost to Procne he did not know. Later he would find out the terrible truth, but not yet. Something was amiss, he felt, even so.

For now Oedipus had his business to pursue. He needed to have the agreement of Tereus to quarter a small contingent of men with their horses for perhaps a couple of weeks in the autumn whilst they waited for the saffron to be brought back down the mountain, before they would escort the precious cargo onwards to Thebes. Tereus was concerned to know the size of the force of men and how they might be paid for and indeed their animals fed. Behind this question Oedipus also detected the wariness that a ruler might feel in having foreign men stationed in his city. Oedipus played upon the new threat being posed by a resurgent Orchomenos – a threat no less to Daulis than to Thebes. An arrangement between their cities was timely, and Oedipus would attempt to see that Tereus would be compensated by goods from Thebes which Daulis lacked. He finally suggested that whilst perhaps some twenty men might be quartered there, not all need stay the whole time and some could meanwhile return to Thebes. Tereus was happy enough with these discussions, and soon enough the two men were able to turn to wider matters over plates of roast meat. Oedipus left the next morning with little further thought of Procne. He was more concerned with having arranged the safety of the saffron trade in the autumn.

The time soon came round when Eudemus reappeared, not only with Alexander but with two attendants and a string of fine horses, all carrying substantial loads of splendid Corinthian potware. They had come over the Gulf via Kreusis and lodged in Thebes for a night before the party was to set out the next morning for Daulis. It was early when the group gathered together in the palace courtyard and the mornings were already chill. Oedipus and a party of twenty young men were all fully armed. He felt it important to give a clear signal to Minyas that any interference with their mission was going to be firmly resisted. The armed guard, each mounted, carried in every case a spear tipped with an iron point and their belts held a short iron sword. Their protection consisted of a round shield made of bronze, wood and leather, and they wore a bronze breastplate and helmet. Eudemus was impressed, and Oedipus himself was quietly satisfied with his force as it rode down into the fields below the city and turned towards Haliartos.

Oedipus was again reckoning to get to Daulis by the late afternoon. The horses with their cargoes of pots would have to travel quite slowly and could not be rushed. All went smoothly until after Haliartos, when as had happened the previous autumn to

Eudemus and Alexander a group of some six horsemen rode up and demanded to know what they were carrying. Oedipus took the lead, and told them that they were on the way from Thebes to Parnassos for the saffron crop and that in accordance with his discussions with Minyas he would not accept any interference or demands for any levy, in either direction.

One of the Orchomenians was recognisable from the earlier visit to the city, and he responded: 'King Oedipus, I remember the discussions with King Minyas well. He required a tax of one-tenth of the crop and we shall expect this when you return. I am sure you will not want hostilities between our two cities.'

Oedipus was not moved by this. 'Tell King Minyas that we shall deal with any threats that you are unwise enough to present to us,' he said and pressed his horse onwards.

The Theban party rode on, eventually leaving the Copais marsh behind, and reached Daulis. There the Corinthian traders continued on towards the Branching Road to reach the upland area, whilst

Oedipus left half his small force in place and led the remainder back towards Thebes.

He was concerned by the possibility of armed conflict with Orchomenos. Once home he called an assembly of the leading families to ensure he had their support if necessary for a larger force to be deployed. He proposed that he took a further twenty armed men back with him to Daulis, so that he would have a party of forty to face down any possible attack by Minyas. The assembly agreed, even though it would mean that many of them or their sons would be involved, with the resulting danger to their lives. The overwhelming view was that Orchomenos would need to be kept in its place, if necessary by the use of force, otherwise the position of Theban trade would be compromised. A small levy on agricultural products was one thing, but on the new saffron trade another.

In a little under two weeks the larger force set out once again. This time they were not encumbered by a string of horses carrying cargo, and they made good time without interference. The problem was going to be on the return trip. First, Oedipus had to deal with

Tereus at Daulis. The Theban force was now forty men strong, with their horses. King Tereus needed mollifying and indeed needed promises of goods as compensation. Oedipus had always found the Davliot king a little difficult to deal with; Tereus was sensitive about his position, although Oedipus was not aware of any threats to it, but he was also defensive about Procne and Philomela and overly anxious to justify his taking the younger sister as his wife. The Theban king did not understand this, since if Procne had died – as Tereus maintained – there seemed little problem. However it was on this visit to Daulis that Oedipus finally understood the true cause of Tereus' unease.

Unlike his men, Oedipus was quartered in the palace. It was a large building which spread over a good part of one end of the acropolis. The servants' quarters were situated furthest from the imposing entrance. Oedipus had no real reason to go into that area of the palace, but on the second afternoon whilst Tereus himself was absent Oedipus needed a herbal remedy for some insect bites on his arm. He could find no one to ask and so ended up wandering into the labyrinth of small rooms in the servants' quarters until he came upon two women working at looms.

He asked about the lotion he required without at first paying too much attention to the pair. One of them replied, whilst the other remained silent. As he glanced at this second woman he thought he recognised her. Although he had only seen her on one previous occasion in the past, she looked very like Procne. He enquired who she was, but she could only make an unintelligible sound in reply. She seemed to be dumb, and Oedipus wondered what fate had befallen her, what it was that Tereus had inflicted on her to ensure her silence. It was this awful history that Oedipus realised lay like a pall over the palace.

Oedipus was left in a quandary as to what to do about this sad discovery. Plainly Tereus did not want him or similar outsiders to know of Procne's position, otherwise he would not have concocted the fiction that she had died. By asking Tereus about it, Oedipus risked alienating his host. He realised it was another secret like the death of Laius that it was better to keep than to spill.

Fortunately it was the next day that the saffron arrived down from Parnassos, guarded by the small Corinthian contingent with Eudemus and Alexander. This distracted Oedipus from more domestic concerns. The most pressing matter was to ready the Theban horsemen, all forty of them, to escort the precious cargo down onto the Boeotian plain and through the territory of Orchomenos. In practical terms this meant getting past Haliartos and onto the Theban plain itself. Now the convoy would have to move at a slow rate owing to the transport of the many jars of spice, leaving it more exposed to attack.

*

They were able to set off early on the following day. Ten Thebans rode at the front led by Oedipus, twenty at the rear and the final ten spread themselves along either side of the convoy. Again there was no incident until they were most of the way to Haliartos, at a point where the road occupied the narrow land between the foothills of Mount Helicon and the lake. Here they were confronted by a strong-looking force of horsemen, one of whom stood in front of the others. They were blocking the road to Thebes. All were armed in much the same way as the Thebans and somehow they had anticipated their arrival only too precisely. They exceeded the Thebans in numbers although not greatly.

It was none other than Minyas who sat astride his horse in front of the Orchomenians.

'So King Oedipus, now we need to conclude the discussion we had in my palace. Either you agree to pay the tax I proposed upon your cargo or some of you will be lengthening your bodies in the dust of this earth.'

Oedipus replied defiantly. 'Not one of my men will do so. I have the pick of the Theban families with me and they will not be bested by the relics of a ruined city such as yours.' His words were designed to provoke his adversary. 'Minyas, the time for discussion is over. Either let us pass in peace or you will need to force us to yield what you claim.' At this point Oedipus told the Thebans to draw up behind him so as to protect the Corinthian party who sat at the rear.

Minyas turned round and approached his men before riding forward again.

'Oedipus, this is an argument which affects both our cities and their wealth. But it is you and I who have taken the positions we have. I suggest that we contest the issue between ourselves. We do not want to inflict untimely Death upon our noble families. Whoever wins the fight between the two of us can dictate the terms to the others.'

Oedipus still wanted clarity. 'If I win, then the trade to Thebes of all goods including the saffron goes free. If I lose, then we pay one-tenth. Is that what you mean?'

All this was shouted between the two men.

The ruler of Orchomenos nodded. 'Yes, we are agreed.'

With that the two men wheeled away, and started circling one another on their horses with their spears held high ready to cast at the other. Minyas was the first to throw his spear, and it went truly and very quickly straight for the neck of Oedipus who was only just able at the last moment to raise his shield and deflect the weapon harmlessly onto the ground.

At that moment the Theban let go his spear and it too clattered against the breastplate of Minyas without wounding him. Both men quickly jumped down from their horses and closed upon each other with their swords. Oedipus was more circumspect and naturally moved less rapidly, whilst the young king of Orchomenos was the more impetuous of the two.

He sprang at Oedipus wielding his sword above his head and attempted to strike down at him. But the Theban king was too quick and plunged his own sword deep into his opponent's midrift below the breast plate as he came forward, and Minyas fell on his knees clutching at the blade, his blood seeping through his fingers onto the dust.

At this point an older man rushed out from amongst the Orchomenians. He ran towards Oedipus and attempted to strike him with his spear. Oedipus seized the shaft of the weapon.

'Why do you break the terms of my agreement with Minyas?' he shouted. 'He has paid for his arrogance with his life. Do you want to add to those going down to Hades this day?'

The older man said nothing, but attempted to remove his sword from his belt and was intent on killing the Theban if he could. Oedipus withdrew his own sword from Minyas and for the second time that day plunged the weapon into his assailant, this time into his neck, and again the blood spurted, just as it had done when he had killed his father years before. The old man crashed to the ground, and his spirit left his body.

There was no further sound and no one spoke. The two men lay dead on the earth. Oedipus stood sword in hand above them. Finally he invited the Orchomenians to take them away for burial.

'We are done,' he said.

It was a sombre procession that passed through Haliartos and on towards Thebes. There was no feeling of triumph among the Thebans, especially on the part of Oedipus. He had killed two men, one of them the same sort of age as his father was at the Schist Road. And he knew not what trouble this was likely to cause in the future.

He had killed the young king of Orchomenos, and his mind dwelt also on the old man whose throat he had cut. He wondered at his identity, and could not help comparing this slaughter with that which he had carried out those years before. He rode on in silence and greeted Epicaste with barely a word when he arrived home at the palace, paying little attention either to his two little boys, Eteocles and Polynices, who ran about before him.

Over the next few days there were practical matters to attend to including the distribution of the saffron and how best the Theban traders might profit from the spice trade. Some of it was to return to Corinth with Eudemus and Alexander. It was a new beginning, albeit one baptised in blood.

However the king played little part and kept himself as best he could to one side. Much of the time he remained in his own rooms, pacing up and down. After several days of this he sent one of his attendants whom he knew had connections in Orchomenos to enquire who was the older man who had died in the fight. The attendant later returned and told him that the man had been a guardian to Minyas and had brought him up as his own son after Minyas' father had died years before in a raiding party.

It turned out Oedipus had in effect killed another father. His mood further darkened.

CHAPTER 11

Two days later the Corinthians left for home, but Oedipus found himself plunged into a form of depression. He had attempted to govern Thebes justly and with a sense of purpose, confident in the proud city's historic past and its destiny as one of the most important places in Greece. He had, he thought, been entirely justified to stand his ground against the ambitions of Minyas and to resist the unfair imposition of taxes upon Theban trade. But in doing so, he had now brought about the deep enmity of Orchomenos by killing its ruler and another important citizen. He feared a much wider war with his neighbour.

However, worse than these fears was the guilt engulfing him, as the killing of Minyas and his father (as Minyas had clearly regarded him) had brought back into his mind the events at the Schist Road. The recent memory of thrusting his sword into the neck of the older man at Haliartos was only too reminiscent of the way he had killed Laius at the crossroads. He felt the gods had conspired to cause him to re-enact the crime against his own father, even if he was justified in killing Minyas' guardian. He could see the blood spilling from the old man's wound much as it had done from his father's. The images became jumbled, and in both cases he sought in his own mind to justify his actions to himself. He had no alternative in either case, he argued – surely he had to defend himself against attack. Yet with Laius the position was not so clear. Laius had no sword, and perhaps the younger man could have retreated rather than slain him. But his anger had got the better of him and he had butchered his father as he scrambled for his spear on the ground. He knew it was his father, and yet he did not stay his hand. It was the sin of parricide.

He had largely buried this memory and its shame beneath the other later events as he became king and established his rule in Thebes. He had sought to rid himself of such guilt as he felt by his frequent visits to the Temple of Dionysos and the libations for his father's shade, and had allowed himself to think that, with his secret secure, there was nothing to fear. However the Erinyes, the furies, came to haunt him. They disturbed his sleep with nightmares, and night after night he was restless as he saw images of Laius lying bleeding on the ground and of his unburied body being picked at by vultures. The three old hags appeared in his dreams as they prodded him with scourges. Oedipus knew who these creatures were, but he did not know how to placate them. As he tossed and turned at night, sometimes shouting out in his sleep, Epicaste would wake up and ask what was troubling him, but he could not share this with his wife, however much he loved her. It was a struggle within him that at times threatened to overwhelm his sanity.

Meanwhile the business of government had to continue, and wearily and often with lack of sleep Oedipus dealt with the day-to-day problems of the city. The most pressing was the question of Orchomenos. As it was now approaching winter, further major hostilities were unlikely, but the question remained as to the future. Theban trade was not being harried as it passed through the territory to the north, but no one knew what might happen in the spring when travel was more frequent.

Once again Oedipus relied on the good sense of Antipoenus. He suggested a council of the important men in Thebes be called to debate the problem. There was no shortage of solutions put forward. The more bellicose of the Theban nobles thought they should assemble a large force and proceed against Orchomenos straightaway whilst its leadership was disrupted. But few among those present had the stomach for hostilities unless their own city or its interests were threatened. And it was possible that Orchomenos had been dealt a blow which would deter them from any further interference anyway. Antipoenus proposed that once again his son be sent as a herald to discuss another meeting between the two sides with a view to agreeing a formal treaty so as to prevent further warfare. However, generous as this offer was, Oedipus was concerned for the safety of the young man in the present heightened atmosphere, even though his person as a herald was meant to be inviolate. It was too early for such an initiative, he felt.

Another issue debated was the threat posed by Orchomenos possibly attempting to clear the sinkholes which might permit the drainage of the Copais marsh. Everyone was aware that with the vast area of land which would then come under cultivation Orchemenos could indeed restore its former position as a major city and competitor to Thebes. No one wished to see that. Yet with its potential revenues from taxation disrupted how could the city realistically set about such a complex project?

At this point one of the older of those present recalled the ancient fortress of Kastro, a huge walled area now deserted, which lay to the east of Orchomenos. He pointed out that Kastro had probably once guarded the important strategic area in the north-east of the Copais basin where it could safeguard the channels and sinkholes which removed the waters of the lake away from the land. His proposal was that in the spring they could send a small force of men to take up a position on this fortress from where they could monitor developments. Kastro could just as easily be used to guard the present situation where the waters were blocked from exiting the lake as it was used formerly to protect the free flow of the water.

In the end Oedipus was happy to agree to a policy of 'wait and see'. The city of Orchomenos was weakened at present and in any event it was now approaching winter. The position could be assessed again in the spring. This was wise. As time went on, word had it that with the death of Minyas the city of Orchomenos had slipped back into mediocrity. At no point again, at least during the time of Oedipus as king of Thebes, did Orchomenos challenge his city, and the Copais basin remained a seasonal swamp of little value. The saffron trade was unhindered, and the traders in Thebes profited.

The position of Oedipus as king was by now well established. He had extended the palace and his family was growing. Epicaste had produced first the two boys Eteocles and Polynices and now two girls, Antigone and Ismene. The city prospered, and his own lands produced a healthy surplus. Yet he remained disturbed by his dreams, and no amount of libations at the temple cleansed his mind. He was still tortured by images of his father dying under his hand at the Schist Road. At times his mood was so dark that he remained in his rooms for days, and neither Epicaste nor little Antigone, his favourite child, could coax him forth.

It was this period that he started visiting another temple, that of Ismenian Apollo, on a hill just outside the walls of the city, named after the river Ismenion which flowed below the sanctuary. It was the god Apollo who had sent him to Thebes from Delphi, and it was the same god whom his father was going to consult when they met at the Branching Road. Moreover it was Apollo's prophesy that had caused Laius to expose him as a child. The deity had played a role at all these important stages of his life, and he now turned to him for some relief from his anxiety and from the Erinyes. Perhaps by regular attendance at his temple and with frequent libation and sacrifice Oedipus could make amends for his sin, since Apollo as a new god among the Greek pantheon had a growing reputation as promoting purification and penance for the expiation of crime and for discouraging vengeance.

And so Oedipus, to the surprise of many around him including Epicaste, became a frequent visitor to Apollo's sanctuary, where in addition to conventional libations he brought boughs of laurel and dedicated a finely wrought tripod. Unlike Delphi, the temple had no priestess and it had yet to develop a reputation for prophesy, but the Theban ruler now wanted no more prophesy – he wanted relief from the furies and some form of redemption.

However the gods had further trials for Oedipus. Eudemus, on one of his visits to Thebes from Corinth, told him of the deaths of both Polybus and Merope. The old king had died first, but Merope had followed her husband to Hades not long afterwards, overwhelmed by her grief. Oedipus reflected how he had not taken the time to travel to Corinth to see his adoptive parents – indeed he had not seen them since just before his marriage to Epicaste all those years before. He could justify this by telling himself that it was difficult for a king to leave his city behind, with all the opportunities for mischief that this presented to those advocating a more collective form of government – as was happening in other parts of Greece (and was to happen in Corinth).

But this did not console him. His loss was real and felt enormous. All his parents were gone, both adoptive and from birth, and such was his sense of guilt that it ate like a worm into his brain. He had killed his own father, and his mother Jocaste had died soon afterwards, unable to live without Laius. Now he felt that his absence from Corinth had probably hastened the deaths of Polybus and Merope, who had died in effect childless and lonely, without the comfort and hope that would have resulted from their son taking over the rule of that great city. Not even his love of Epicaste and his devotion to his young children could distract him from his inner turmoil. Wherever he turned there was loss, and yet he saw that it was he who had brought it about.

It was the strange figure of Teiresias who brought some comfort to Oedipus, initially at least. The king encountered him on one of his visits to the sanctuary of Apollo. Teiresias appeared ageless, neither young nor old, attired in a simple white tunic, someone who seemed to hover between the world of men and of gods. He looked male and yet there was something delicate and feminine about his movements, as if he was a subtle blend of the two sexes. He appeared to dwell in a part of the sanctuary out of sight to visitors such as Oedipus, yet would materialise in the temple, moving quietly in the shadows of the rudimentary building. So unobstrusive was he that it was some time before Oedipus realised that this mysterious being was completely blind – until he saw his empty eyes he did not know. That was on the first occasion they spoke, when in reply to Oedipus' enquiry Teiresias styled himself as a priest of Apollo, not yet claiming a role as a prophet of the god. That was to come some time later.

Teiresias had not been able to see who was addressing him, but he already knew it was Oedipus and he replied accordingly: 'King Oedipus, you ask who I am. I am Teiresias, the priest of Apollo. What is it that brings you to his sanctuary so often? What is it that is troubling you? Perhaps with my help the lord Apollo will assist you.'

'Teiresias, you will know that I was brought up by the king and queen of Corinth and that I later came to Thebes to find that my true father Laius was dead. My mother Jocaste died not very long afterwards. Now my parents in Corinth have died. I have been orphaned twice over, and my mind finds it difficult to find peace.'

'Lord Oedipus,' replied Teiresias, 'why so? Have you offended the gods by your treatment of your several parents? If you have not, surely your mind should be at rest, even if you are sad at these deaths.'

Oedipus sensed the sharp intelligence and perception at work in the priest and knew that he had to reply carefully, giving an explanation for his agony of mind without revealing the very particular cause of it.

'I fear I did not care sufficiently for my parents in Corinth after I came here, and similarly I did not devote my mother Jocaste enough of my time after I had come back to her from the dead.' He made no reference to Laius.

'You have no reason to feel guilty about those of whom you have spoken. You are a king and have no duties other than to the gods. In your answer you did not speak of Laius but I understand you did not know him,' replied Teiresias.

Oedipus was able to agree this quite truthfully, and Teiresias observed that he therefore could not have failed his father in any way.

'I am but a mere priest of Apollo, but I believe the god will give you peace if you make libations to the spirits of your parents in his temple.'

The king remembered the instruction from the Pythia to worship Dionysos and to honour the ruler of Thebes. He had previously directed most of his libations to the shade of Laius at the temple of Dionyos, but what the Pythia had said did not preclude him from making offerings at the temple of Apollo. Henceforth Oedipus drew comfort from doing so. His mind became easier, perhaps as the events themselves that caused his unrest lay further and further in the past.

On his visits to the sanctuary of Apollo, Oedipus talked frequently with the blind priest. Teiresias had extraordinary stories to tell. One day he told Oedipus that he had spent years as a woman and had even had children. The king found this difficult to believe, yet he could not dispute the man's femininity. He later learnt that on occasions Teiresias, despite his role at Apollo's temple, still dressed as a female worshipper to go up on the mountain to rave with the Bacchants in honour of Dionysos.

Another time he explained that he had been blinded by the goddess Athena as a punishment for seeing her bathe naked. Oedipus could not resist asking what she looked like unclothed, but the priest refused to answer this since he said it would be impious and he did not wish to offend the goddess again. On yet another occasion Teiresias gave a totally different reason for his blindness. He said he had to mediate in a dispute between Zeus and Hera as to who had the greater pleasure during sex, the man or the woman. Zeus said it was the woman and Hera the man. As Teiresias had been both, he was the obvious person to ask. He answered that of ten parts of pleasure, the man enjoys only one. Hera was furious and blinded him.

Oedipus loved these stories, not that he could take them seriously. Not only were the two accounts of his blinding totally at odds with each other, but Teiresias alone amongst mortals that he had met claimed direct experience of the gods. Either he was remarkably privileged or more likely, the king thought, was a fraud or simply crazy. So whilst Oedipus enjoyed talking with Teiresias he was sceptical of his claims. He learnt later to his cost that he should not have been so dismissive, especially when Teiresias began to develop a reputation for augury.

CHAPTER 12

While Oedipus slowly became less preoccupied with the fate of Laius and the deaths of the others that had affected him so badly, his family was growing up. His wife Epicaste had taken prime responsibility for the children, since Oedipus had found it difficult to deal with anything beyond the pressing affairs of the city. The one time he managed to be with his two sons, Eteocles and Polynices, was when they went on boar hunts rather as Polybus had done with him when he was a child in Corinth. The boys had now both reached puberty, a stage when Oedipus felt that they should be learning the manly pursuit of hunting and practising the use of spears.

The older of the two children, Eteocles, was strong, being built much like his father. He was already adept at throwing a spear. But he was also very quick, unhindered by the disability that Oedipus had suffered in his feet. His nature was difficult however. He did not like being told what to do, particularly by his father, whose slightly clumsy gait he even mocked. He was a truculent boy who did not find it easy to mix with others, and he and his brother Polynices were endlessly fighting. His parents feared for Eteocles' future, but neither could have imagined the impact he was to have on their lives, certainly that of Oedipus.

Eteocles displayed his difficult character during the boar hunts. There were several areas on the lower slopes of Mount Helicon where the wild boar could be found. Every time that Oedipus mooted a hunt in a particular location, Eteocles would sulk unless it was the place he wanted to go. The king would brook no such dissent, and so Eteocles often remained out of temper and was especially awkward to deal with. Eventually, on one such occasion, the boy almost caused his father a serious injury. They had gone to a hunting area particularly favoured by Oedipus since it was near Erythrae and the king had fond memories of hunting there with Epicaste's father.

Eteocles wanted to go elsewhere, precisely because his father had chosen this place.

Oedipus and the two boys had travelled there by chariot, and the king had identified a thicket with some boar in it. There was a large male and a female with young, and Oedipus realised the male was likely to be particularly aggressive in guarding them. He had told Polynices to go to the far side and drive the boar out, whilst he and Eteocles were to wait on the side where the animals were likely to emerge.

It took a surprising length of time for the boar to show themselves. When they did, for some reason the female came out ahead of the male and rushed straight at Oedipus, followed by the large male. Oedipus had to spear the first animal as it was almost upon him, and Eteocles should have thrown his spear at the second animal as he had been trained to do. But the lad had disappeared without reason or explanation and left his father to cope on his own. Oedipus having speared the first boar could not extricate his weapon and only with difficulty stopped the much larger male with his short sword as it sprang at him, one of the animal's tusks causing a minor wound to his chest in the process. He was furious, and told Polynices – who had now come round to see the outcome – to go and find Eteocles and bring him to him.

Polynices eventually returned with Eteocles, and Oedipus tore into the older boy, telling him how he had very nearly been seriously wounded by the male boar and demanding to know why he had not stayed where he had been posted.

'But father,' said Eteocles, 'you know I did not want to come to this hunting place, and so I lost interest when it all took time.' His tone was nonchalant and uncaring. 'Besides, you are such a good hunter and so quick,' he said in a mocking tone, 'I knew you did not need my help.'

Oedipus had to stay his hand and step back rather than strike the boy, he was so angry.

'And what if the male had succeeded in piercing my chest with his tusk, it might have killed me. Does that not concern you?'

Eteocles gave no reply initially. But after a time he looked directly at his father and said, 'In time I shall be very happy to be king in your stead.'

He appeared to lack all normal respect for his father and most ordinary feelings. Oedipus never trusted Etcocles again after this incident and did not take him on another boar hunt. He became aware for the first time that, just as he had supplanted his own father, Eteocles might one day seek to do the same.

*

Oedipus still went to the Temple of Apollo from time to time, where he would encounter Teiresias. The priest was beginning to earn a reputation for prophesy, particularly by the interpretation of the images described to him as appearing in the smoke from burnt offerings. There were those that consulted Teiresias as a prophet of Apollo, much as the Pythia was consulted at Delphi. The king was not unhappy at this development as sometimes it was from his own herds that the ox or bullock was purchased for the sacrifice.

The herds and lands belonging to the king had done well over the years. As time went by, his shepherds had increased the numbers of his sheep and goats, indeed he now had several flocks under their charge; his herds of cattle were the biggest in Thebes; his fields supplied a healthy surplus of corn; and his men had grafted many new olive trees on the wild olives on the lower parts of Helicon so that he numbered many hundreds, if not thousands of trees, on his land. His oil supplied all the domestic needs of the palace and a good deal besides. The position of Oedipus himself appeared to be secure, there was no prospect of hostilities with Orchomenos, the city was prospering, all was benign – or so it seemed. The palace itself was well organised under the watchful eye of Epicaste and if one left to one side the baneful presence of Eteocles, the other three children were happy and obedient to their parents. Epicaste herself had retained her beauty and added to it a calm presence which affected those around her, including Oedipus, who was by now much less troubled by his demons.

Yet in the bright, clear sunshine there were shadows, and concealed in the shadows lurked spirits which were determined to emerge into the light and change the landscape. Just as Eteocles was coming of age, disaster struck Thebes. The herds became ill, and a rust consumed the buds and fruits of the earth. Unusual numbers of babies died in the womb. Sickness stalked the streets and the countryside wore a derelict look. It was a plague which no one, not the oldest inhabitant, had witnessed before. The Thebans turned to the altars in the temples bringing boughs of laurel and other offerings, and they sought help from Oedipus, not because they believed he had godly attributes, but because he had acquired a reputation for wisdom and perhaps he alone of mortals might have a solution to this affliction which affected him and the palace no less than everyone else. They besieged the steps of his palace and entreated his help.

Oedipus and those whom he consulted in the city knew no better than any other citizen what to do. He decided that he would approach Teiresias who by now had a reputation for augury. Consequently he went to the Temple of Apollo to approach the priest. As so often in the past the blind priest materialised from the shadows of the dimly lit building, knowing full well it was the king who stood before him.

'King Oedipus,' he said, 'I believe I know what is bringing you here. It is the plague which has descended on the city and your house equally.'

'You are right, as you frequently are, Teiresias. I come on behalf of the city to seek your insight into this calamity. We need to know what is causing the disease and how we might rid ourselves of it.'

Teiresias was silent for a little time. 'I am indeed vexed by this question myself, Oedipus. I suggest you sacrifice one of your oxen and allow me to read what appears from it.'

The king was content to do this. It amounted to a programme of action which might give comfort to the city. The result was that the following day his herdsman brought a young animal to the temple and slit its throat by the altar outside. Oedipus stood by as the animal was butchered and some of the meat roasted. As the flesh from the beast cooked, the smoke rose briskly into the morning air, and Teiresias stood by to interpret any signs and images which could be seen. He could not see these himself and was dependent upon another young servant of the temple to do so. The boy spoke in hushed tones to the blind seer and Oedipus could not hear what was being said. This went on for some time, with the king increasingly concerned as to what was going to come from the prophet.

Teiresias finally spoke. 'There is plague, and the reason is that the land is polluted.'

Oedipus was not impressed by this response. 'That we know, Teiresias. The land is diseased. We want to know the cause of it and how we can cleanse ourselves of the pollution.'

'That I cannot tell you,' the priest said.

'You cannot, or you will not?' replied Oedipus angrily.

'I cannot tell you what I know,' was the answer.

'Teiresias, I have known you now for many years. I have been a faithful follower of our lord Apollo. I am your king in this world, our city is polluted, and you will not tell me what we may do to rid ourselves of this curse.'

'Oedipus, I cannot do that. When you discover what needs to be done, you will understand, but I cannot be the person to tell you this. And perhaps I am wrong and you should seek the answer from the Pythia at Delphi.'

Oedipus was not to be placated by this prevarication. 'You still refuse to tell me what you know?'

There was no reply.

The king had always had an almost ungovernable temper when provoked. It was that which had caused his rash deed at the Schist Road. And his anger spilled over again.

'Teiresias, if you will not do as I bade you to do, to tell me what you know, and if you refuse to bring aid to my city, our city, then I order you from this sanctuary and banish you forever from Thebes.'

Even then, Teiresias did not speak and simply turned and quietly left the temple.

CHAPTER 13

Outside the sanctuary, everyone was anxious to know what had taken place within. Oedipus came out stony-faced and said little beyond the fact that Teiresias had failed to give an answer and had been banished. The Thebans were mystified by what had occurred, or rather what had not occurred – it was unheard of for the prophet of Apollo to fail to give a response when asked, however cryptic and unhelpful. It created a deeper sense of foreboding in the streets of the city as the news spread, and the men stood around uncertainly.

The king returned to the palace and told Epicaste of his conversation with Teiresias. She felt that Oedipus had been over-hasty in banishing the prophet and asked him to reconsider. Her husband usually listened to her and he said he would think further about it.

'What I will do in the first place', he said, 'is to listen to his advice that we should consult Delphi. Epicaste, let us send someone to do that, since at this perilous time I do not think I should leave Thebes.'

Epicaste agreed. She then made a surprising suggestion. 'Let us send Eteocles with an attendant. He is coming of age, and perhaps giving him this responsibility will bend him to the common cause of the city and even our family.'

Oedipus was sceptical. He had as little to do with his eldest son as he could. On the other hand, the plan certainly had the possible benefit that his wife imagined and had the advantage too of keeping Eteocles out of the palace for a few days. He therefore agreed that they would send the young man to enquire of the Pythia what they might do to rid the city of the plague that so afflicted it.

Preparations were quickly made and the following day Eteocles and a servant were ready to set out on horseback for Delphi. Oedipus thought the journey would be easier on horse rather than by chariot, and something in his mind recoiled from the idea of a chariot of the royal house of Thebes being driven again across the crossroads at the Branching Road. He gave Eteocles directions for the journey and told him that he could if necessary take the higher route by Daulis to seek shelter with King Tereus, albeit Tereus was now old and would barely remember any ties with the king of Thebes. Oedipus put to the back of his mind the fate of Queen Procne whom he had last seen in the palace kitchens at Daulis.

It was late summer and it was not long before the last of the corn would normally be taken from the land, except that now the crops were withered and the fields more than usually brown, even black in places. In normal times, in a few weeks they would be looking forward to the arrival of the saffron harvest from Parnassos, but this was not on Oedipus' mind as Eteocles set out. He could only hope that the Pythia would reveal to him what for a reason known only to himself Teiresias had failed to tell Oedipus.

It was an anxious week before Eteocles returned. He came sweeping into the palace and, after refreshing himself from the spring water piped to the basin at the entrance, he straightaway addressed Oedipus in the main hall. He seemed to his father to have grown both in stature and in the maturity of his manner during his absence.

'Father,' he started, 'I have much news to inform you,' and he began an elaborate account of all that had taken place in the last week.

'First I travelled directly to Delphi where I managed to secure a visit to the Pythia on the third morning. I had heard that often the priestess speaks in riddles which others must decipher, but this time she was clear enough. I asked simply how we were to rid the city of Thebes of the plague.

'Her reply was to find the murderer of Laius and to expel him from Thebes. I was greatly concerned at this response since the murder of Laius had occurred before I was born, in fact before you became king, and I could not understand how we were to discover his identity after almost twenty years. I had understood that he had disappeared with his carriage and his attendant somewhere near the crossroads of the Branching Road, or so it had seemed from the enquiries made by the servant sent by the queen within days of Laius' disappearance.

'So it was with little hope that I turned around from Delphi and retraced my tracks to the Branching Road that afternoon. But then I had some good fortune and I discovered that Phocis has begun to give up its secrets. As I approached the crossroads at the bottom of the defile where the three roads meet, I encountered a shepherd who hailed from Daulis but kept his flock in that area. He had a sheepfold nearby and as it was dusk I sought shelter with him. In accordance with the laws of hospitality he happily provided space for myself and my attendant and we tethered the horses nearby.

'After he had shared some simple food with us, we talked about the plague in Thebes and the purpose of our journey to the Pythia. He was a wise man and did not rush to tell us what he knew.

'Then he started. "I believe I know where King Laius met his end, together with his attendant. A few years ago I was speaking with a shepherd from Ambrossos who had a shelter for his animals on the other side of the large pile of stones at the base of the defile just below us. He told me that he had seen with his own eyes the remains of a man with a fine red cloak lying under the stones but whose body had been partly disturbed, most probably by the jackals that haunt these hills and cause our dogs to bark much of the night. He later showed me the place, and there I could still see parts of the skeleton of the man protruding from one side of the pile of stones. The partial skeleton of a second person was just visible nearby. By then we did know of the disappearance of the king of Thebes, somewhere along the road to Delphi. And what convinced me that these were probably the bones of the king was another thing told to me by this same shepherd."

'The man paused and at this point offered us a glass of crude wine from a large flagon at the back of his low dwelling. He took one himself and, refreshed, continued with his account.

'His informant, the shepherd from Ambrossos, had told him that one day, when he was on his way with his sheep from the village, he had walked into the holm oak to look for a ewe which had strayed from the path. There he said he had seen amongst the small trees what was left of a substantial chariot, its wheels and base already rotting. There was no sign of any animal or human parts there. The horses must have freed themselves, or perhaps the chariot had been found with the horses still joined and only the animals were led away because the chariot would have been too obvious a prize.'

Oedipus was shaken by this news. He remembered his father in his red cloak standing in the chariot, and he remembered too how he sent the chariot off with the horses in the direction of Ambrossos. But he was reluctant to accept that Laius had been found, as this was the first step in the possible revelation of his terrible secret. However, he stayed calm and asked how it was that the shepherd was so sure that this was King Laius.

Eteocles continued: 'The shepherd to whom we spoke realised that the remains were those of a wealthy man as could be seen by his cloak and it seemed natural that such a man would have been travelling by chariot. The two together – what was left of the man (and perhaps an attendant) and the carriage – suggested they had been killed at the crossroads and hastily buried. The chariot had gone down the road towards Ambrossos.'

'But why must it have been Laius?' pursued Oedipus.

Eteocles agreed there was no certain proof from these discoveries alone, but he had more to tell.

'The following morning the shepherd took us to see the place where he had seen the skeletons. They were gone, but there was still a small piece of the red cloth visible on the ground, the corner of which was pinned down by a large stone. The jackals must have taken the bones.'

'Was there any sign of the chariot?' asked Oedipus.

'That was more difficult. The shepherd from Daulis had not seen this himself, and told us that the only way to find any traces of it would be to speak to the other shepherd from Ambrossos in case he could still locate it. And he took us along the track in the direction of the village to try to find him. After walking halfway to the village leading our horses, we did indeed come across the second shepherd minding a large flock on the hillside. To my surprise he said he knew exactly where the surviving parts of the carriage were to be found. We said goodbye to the

Davliot, and the second shepherd led us some distance through the holm oak until we finally came across the wreckage. The wheels were still largely intact, though the rest of it had mostly disintegrated. There was one thing however which convinced me that this was indeed Laius' chariot.'

'What was that?' Oedipus asked quickly.

'On the piece of wood which survived from the front of the carriage, there was roughly carved the head of our god, Dionysos. It was much the same as the heads which are still engraved on our royal chariots.'

CHAPTER 14

I t was going to be difficult for Oedipus to refuse
to accept the obvious fact which he of course
knew to be true, that Laius had indeed been
killed and buried at the crossroads. If he tried to
debate it with Eteocles, it would only perhaps draw
suspicion upon him, given that it was known that he
had arrived at the palace in Thebes from Delphi not
many days afterwards. As yet there was nothing to
suggest his involvement.

So he complimented his son on his discovery.
'Eteocles, you have done well to find out where King
Laius was buried and indeed therefore where he was
probably killed. We are however no nearer to
discovering the murderer and then cleansing our land
of the pollution. Perhaps the truth is indeed what was
rumoured, that he was killed by brigands who were

lying in wait at the Branching Road where travellers on their way to Delphi were bound to pass.'

Eteocles remained quiet at this point, and Oedipus fondly hoped that his son could shed no further light on the identity of the murderer. It was hard to see how he might, since the king was convinced there was no witness to the killing. Oedipus went to ask therefore what else could Eteocles report.

The young man continued: 'We retraced our steps to the crossroads and were debating what we should do about perhaps moving more stones and possibly reburying any remains of King Laius, when a remarkable thing happened. First we saw a huge eagle circling above us, but this suddenly took flight as a great black cloud descended the defile behind. Then there was a huge clap of thunder, followed by lightning, and within moments the heavens opened and we were lashed by a storm, first with hailstones the size of hens' eggs and then with driving rain which drenched us. I remembered your suggestion that we might obtain shelter if necessary with King Tereus in Daulis. And so we remounted our horses and took ourselves off to that city as quickly as they would take us.'

'And did King Tereus offer you shelter and hospitality as I would expect him to do?'

'When we arrived at Daulis', Eteocles continued, 'we made our way to the palace and were eventually taken to the king. He is old and I am sure he can be difficult at times, but he was kind enough, particularly after I told him that you were my father and you had sought shelter that time years before when you were journeying from Delphi and went on to solve the problem of the Sphinx before arriving at Thebes. He offered us a room for the night and invited us to dine with him that evening.

'After we had dried ourselves and rested, he provided us with a good enough meal. There was roasted meat and he produced wine from his own vines. He said he now remembered your visit well for a particular reason.

'You too had arrived, he said, after a huge local downpour and you too were wet. He said it was a local phenomenon which occurred once or twice a year when the clouds gathered at the Branching

Road, having been siphoned down the defile from the direction of Delphi. It battered any travellers first with hailstones and then driving rain. Do you remember that, father?'

Oedipus had done his best to put the detailed events of that fatal day out of his mind, but when reminded of it, he could see it clearly enough in his memory. He recalled that the cloud had descended on him after the encounter when he was debating what to do and where to go, and he had been soaked.

'I do remember it vaguely, yes, though those times are overlaid by other memories, such as my encounter with the Pythia and Tereus' preoccupation with Philomela. Did you see Tereus' queen?' Oedipus asked Eteocles, moving the subject away from his visit twenty years before.

'I saw none of his family. It seems there is none to be seen. He remarked at one point that he was now on his own, having lost first Procne and then his second wife Philomela. In addition his son, Itys, was dead, and I did not like to ask how that occurred.

'There was another strange thing. When that evening I walked around the acropolis there were more swallows than I have ever seen in one place before, and I heard the nightingale sing, more beautifully than ever I had previously known. It was as if Daulis was being given over to the birds. And the oddest thing of all is that King Tereus himself was wearing a cloak of black and white, and with his long pointed nose he reminded me of a hoopoe which I once saw in the fields at Erythrae.'

Oedipus reflected back on his sad encounter with Procne and wondered now too about the fates of Philomela and Itys, but he had more pressing things on his mind. The plague was still ravaging the land and city of Thebes. Yet if his exposure as the murderer of Laius was to be the cure, that was not a solution he could contemplate. There was nothing as yet to point to his own involvement in Laius' death. He could only hope that somehow the problem would go away, the crops would miraculously recover and the murderer of Laius would remain the mystery which it should.

It was not to be. Oedipus had thanked his son for his help, assuming that Eteocles would feel that he had nothing further to accomplish. But the young man now acted as if he was on a mission to discover the truth of Laius' fate.

'Father,' he said, 'I want to talk further to the servant whom Jocaste had sent out to look for Laius, in case there is some detail that might shed light on the murder. Perhaps the sighting of a strange traveller or group of travellers at the time.'

Oedipus tried to deflect this, precisely for the reason that Eteocles wished to pursue it.

'I am not sure that he still works in the palace and perhaps he is no longer alive,' he temporised.

Eteocles was not so easily diverted and told Oedipus that he had spoken to the man's son who now worked at the palace in the place of his father who had become a shepherd. It was from the son that Eteocles had heard the account of the investigations undertaken by the man at the behest of Jocaste, when Laius was first missing. Eteocles said he would send for the older man, so that they could hear from him first-hand.

It was the following day that the shepherd, as he now was, attended the palace. He was already quite old and was worn by a life in the elements after choosing to leave the palace's comforts. Both Eteocles and Oedipus were present as he gave his account. At first he had difficulty casting his mind back to his various conversations so many years ago. But he got into his stride and remembered the accounts he heard clearly enough – in particular one of the sight of Laius and his chariot given by the shepherd from Panopeos whom he met by the spring in Tseresi. It was a vivid description of the king riding past with his red cloak streaming behind him. Eteocles asked the old man if at any point in his enquiries there was any description of a solitary traveller or for that matter any band of brigands who might have encountered Laius in the area of the Schist Road. Nothing came of this, and it looked as if little would be added to what was already known.

Then Eteocles had a moment of inspiration. Did his informant tell him if the weather was normal the afternoon when he had seen the king travel past in his chariot. The old man thought for a while, as if he was scrolling through the visual images he could summon up from the day he talked to the shepherd in Tseresi so many years before.

He suddenly became animated. 'I remember now. The shepherd told me there had been a huge thunderstorm over by the crossroads later that afternoon. He said the clouds often gather just there and then you get hail and heavy rain. He had been concerned whether the chariot had gone up the defile towards Delphi before the storm hit – the rain would have made the track at the crossroads impassable for a time.'

Eteocles looked immediately at his father. 'You experienced a thunderstorm and hail and rain at those crossroads, didn't you, father?'

Oedipus' heart jumped. 'Yes but I understand it is a local phenomenon, which occurs from time to time,' he said quickly.

Eteocles did not let go so easily. He asked the old man if the shepherd from Panopeos said more about these local storms.

'He did say that they weren't that common, and that is why he had remembered this particular storm on this occasion,' the old man replied.

He could give no further help and left the room. Eteocles turned now to look steadfastly at his father.

'Father,' he said in all apparent innocence at first, 'you arrived at Thebes within days of the disappearance of Laius at the crossroads as we now know. The afternoon that the king must have vanished at the crossroads, in fact when he must have been killed there, there was a heavy thunderstorm in that area. It must have been the same thunderstorm that you experienced in the region before travelling to Daulis. There was no other such storm at that time.'

Oedipus asked what his son was now saying.

Eteocles simply enquired of his father, 'Didn't you see Laius and his chariot on the road?'

The older man denied doing so. His heart was now beating wildly and his head was beginning to ache, much as it used to do when he was tormented by the furies.

Eteocles would not stop and was like a hound after a strong scent.

'Father, you were coming from Delphi, whilst Laius was going in the opposite direction. You turned left to travel to Daulis, as we know. You didn't see Laius in the defile above that turning, did you?'

Oedipus now remained quiet.

'The shepherd from Panopeos thought Laius had enough time to get to the Branching Road before the storm, and the storm hit you in that area. Yet you did not see Laius above the crossroads. Well, you would not have done, because he was in fact killed at the crossroads. Laius must have reached the Branching Road at about the time you did. Father, are you sure you did not encounter him there?'

The king was now white. 'Are you now alleging that your father has committed the sin of parricide?' he asked slowly.

'Are you denying this?' Eteocles replied.

Oedipus shook his head.

His son continued: 'If you still deny it, there is one man who will know the truth. The prophet whom you tried to banish – Teiresias. My mother had him recalled, and I shall now seek him out at the Temple of Apollo. Let us go together.'

Oedipus was now in the grip of his own fate and he stumbled blindly towards it.

CHAPTER 15

As the two men walked the short distance to the Temple of Apollo, they said little. The mind of Oedipus was very disturbed. He not only recalled the events at the crossroads but this was overlaid by the same feelings of guilt and terror that the furies had inflicted on him those years before and which came flooding back into his head. Eteocles by contrast was in an elated mood. He believed he had finally discovered how his father had become king of Thebes, and he realised that the moment was drawing near when he himself may play the same role of displacing the king. Was it not the natural sequence of events, he thought with satisfaction. And he, unlike his father, had not committed a grave crime in order to do so.

They found the temple empty at first, but as had often happened in the past Teiresias appeared as if some invisible cord had gently pulled him into the building. The blind prophet needed no prompting. He knew who was in front of him.

'King Oedipus,' he said addressing him directly, 'the queen requested that I return after you banished me from my home, and I have done as she asked. What do you seek of me now?'

Eteocles spoke first. 'It is I, Eteocles, the son of the king, who asks you this. Are you aware of the answer that the Pythia gave me when I asked the priestess how we might rid ourselves of the scourge affecting our city?'

Teiresias replied: 'Of course, Eteocles. As Apollo's priest and prophet I know his responses. The Pythia bade you to find and expel the murderer of Laius from Thebes.'

He then turned to Oedipus. 'I knew this was what our lord Apollo was saying when you sought my help before, King Oedipus. You know very well why I could not tell you this myself.'

Again, as Oedipus remained silent, Eteocles intervened.

'We need you to name the murderer, Teiresias, since all the evidence points to the king himself and he will not admit he committed this dreadful offence. The city cannot be cleansed until this is done and the murderer is expelled,' Eteocles said.

Some part of Oedipus remained defiant. Was he really to be brought low by his own son? Did he deserve such a fate for punishing Laius when his father had transgressed all decent laws by exposing his son as an infant?

'I do not accept any guilt for the murder of Laius,' he said quietly.

Eteocles seized on this and asked him, 'Do you then accept that you killed Laius at the Branching Road?'

Oedipus said slowly, 'There was an altercation...' and then he trailed off.

There was silence as those words hung in the fetid air in the temple.

It was broken finally by Eteocles. 'So at last my father has admitted the killing, Teiresias. You knew this all along. Must he not be expelled from the city in accordance with the words of Apollo?'

The fate of Oedipus was now in the hands of Teiresias, the very man whom the king had himself chosen to banish from Thebes only a short time ago. The priest was hardly likely to set himself against the response of the Pythia and suggest a different course to that which the lord Apollo wished and which the king's son was only too keen to see come to pass.

Yet Teiresias had a residual loyalty to Oedipus whom he had come to respect, if not hugely like, over the many years when the king had sought solace from his troubled mind in the temple.

At this fateful point he hesitated. 'I believe that at such an important moment in the history of our great city we should take care to make a correct decision in accordance with the wishes of the gods. I think we should consult Lord Apollo one further time as to what we should do.'

Eteocles would have none of that. 'But, Teiresias, the Pythia was clear. We have found the murderer and he should be expelled from the city!'

'Are you so sure', the priest responded, 'that you would want your father to wander without a home for the rest of his life? Beware, lest a similar or worse fate befall yourself, with no one to offer you pardon and forgiveness for your own mistakes.'

The young man was not to be persuaded, so determined was he to seize control from his father. But Teiresias had the authority as the prophet of Apollo to overrule him and he simply stated that he intended to view the images from the smoke of a burnt sacrifice to see the way ahead.

Oedipus had become a passive spectator of events. He could only wait upon the outcome of the augury that Teiresias intended to conduct. He felt hounded by misfortune. At one time he appeared to have a gilded youth, the child of not one but two kingdoms, who had secured the throne of a renowned ancient city for himself and his family.

But that world had crumbled as his guilty secret had been revealed by something as simple as the observation of a thunderstorm. He could only see himself being driven from his kingdom, without even the opportunity to defend himself, so perpetuating the cycle of father and son rivalry. He could see, even if Eteocles could not, that his son was probably only storing up more difficulties for his own future if this was to continue.

Meanwhile Teiresias' assistant had obtained the remains of an animal freshly slaughtered that day, not all of which had been used in earlier sacrifice. Teiresias recognised the urgency of the present situation and the need to give an answer to the question of Oedipus' expulsion from the city. He was therefore prepared to break with the normal practice of requiring a fresh victim on the occasion of each sacrifice, since this time, unusually, it was he who was consulting the god.

It was already dusk as the fire gathered heat on the altar outside the temple and the smoke began to rise, billowed by a light wind that was now blowing across the city. Oedipus and Eteocles remained at some distance as was required of supplicants, whilst the priest and his assistant stood near the altar.

The white tufts of smoke rose in detached patches at first, uncombined and meaningless, until they suddenly came together and formed a distinctive shape. It was the figure of a man, larger than normal wearing what appeared to be a wreath of laurel. The daylight was fading but the form became more visible as its outline was lit by the flames of the fire below. It then moved and as it did so Oedipus and Eteocles instinctively raised their hands towards it. Teiresias could not see the image but could be heard to say 'Lord Apollo' whilst his assistant stood transfixed and stayed silent.

The god appeared to point towards Oedipus, and a disembodied voice could be heard above the crackling of the flames, clear but distant.

'Oedipus, you have offended the gods by killing your father. By normal rules you should be expelled from the city.'

No one spoke, certainly not Oedipus who now bowed his head.

Apollo continued: 'But we are not unjust. Laius had himself offended against the laws by exposing you as a child, and you have been a good king. I grant you the freedom to remain as ruler provided that you give my worship precedence in Thebes. Your son must yet bide his time before he replaces you.'

Oedipus never knew how this extraordinary event occurred. He could not judge whether Apollo had indeed finally revealed himself and his own scepticism was entirely misplaced, or whether Teiresias had engineered this theatrical outcome. It fortunately did not matter. If it was indeed the god that had spoken, as he was prepared to believe, that was the end of it. If it was a trick of Teiresias himself, no one was going to seek to overturn the decision, blessed as it was by the priest and prophet of Apollo.

The one person aggrieved was Eteocles, but there was nothing he could do. The city had its answer to the problem of the plague. Oedipus was to give ascendancy to Apollo and be assiduous in his worship. The king was forced to live with his secret exposed for all to see. But Eteocles would have to wait, for another opportunity, if or when it came. The wheel had not completed its circle.

AFTERWORD

This is therefore far from the traditional ending as for example we find in Sophocles' version. There once the truth is known, in fact discovered by Oedipus' own persistent enquiry into past events, Jocaste hangs herself and Oedipus strikes out his own eyes. He is then driven from the kingdom and Eteocles becomes king, with the further chaos that ensues owing to war with his brother Polynices.

However in the Odyssey, the poet Homer, long before Sophocles, has Oedipus continuing to rule at Thebes and this allows for a different ending. According to Book 11, Odysseus descends into the underworld and there he sees the mother of Oedipus, whom Homer calls Epikaste (but we know as Jocaste).

Odysseus recounts this to the Phaiacians:

And I saw the mother of Oedipus, beautiful Epikaste,

who in the ignorance of her mind did a
   monstrous thing
by marrying her own son: he, after killing his
   father,
married her. The gods presently made this
   known among men.
But while he suffered pains in much-loved
   Thebes
he yet reigned over the Thebans through the
   will of the gods…
(Odyssey 11. 271-276, translated by the
   author)

There is a passing reference to the same effect in
the Iliad. So, whilst Homer like Sophocles has
Oedipus marrying his mother (and that is certainly a
common theme in antiquity), Oedipus does not blind
himself nor does he have to go into exile, as happens
so poignantly in Euripides' Phoenissae. He continues
as king of Thebes. In that situation we can only
imagine the accommodations he would have to make
to expiate his crime.

In the traditional story it was always the marriage to his mother that I found unnecessary. I address this question further below. But by making Oedipus aware that Laius is his father and that it is him whom he has killed at the Branching Road we can then avoid an incestuous relationship with his mother. What I found interesting was that by giving Oedipus the knowledge of his true birth we can watch where the ramifications of this end, rather like dropping a pebble into a pond and seeing the ripples spread. One of the consequences is that, since there is no incest with his mother, it becomes more credible that Oedipus can remain as king of Thebes.

In the Author's Note I speak of the story being principally about the perennial rivalry between fathers and sons, the death of the former and the replacement by the latter. This is a recurrent theme of Greek myth, most graphically when Chronos emasculates his father Uranus and then rules in his stead, only in turn to be usurped by Zeus. We do not perhaps need to go so far as to see the murder of Laius as a record of the solar king's ritual death at the hands of his successor, as Robert Graves suggests in Greek Myths Vol 2 105.2. Nor on the other hand do we need to see Oedipus as a Hellenic or Greek invader of Thebes who suppressed the old Minoan cult of the mother goddess, as Robert Graves also suggested. The recent debate about a patriarchal society replacing a matriarchal one turns out to be sterile, with little evidence in its favour, certainly in mainland Greece. Similarly there is no clear evidence of a matrilineal law of succession being substituted by a patrilineal law. The desire of sons to emulate and surpass or surplant their fathers appears to have a degree of universal truth without more. That is how I prefer to see the Oedipus myth.

I cannot deny that the marriage between Oedipus and his mother is a fixed part of the traditional myth, whether in Homer or in works of the later classical authors. And it is tempting to see in this, as Freud did, another apparent universal truth – namely the alleged instinctive desire of men to sleep with their mothers. However there is a fundamental flaw in this: Oedipus did not know that Jocaste was his mother. That is what gave rise to the ultimate problem and what caused his revulsion. So strong was the sense of guilt at having committed incest that in Sophocles' play not only does Oedipus blind himself but Jocaste commits suicide. These are the direct consequences for an innocent man who did not know what he was doing, which is indeed the very essence of a Greek tragedy.

This is a long way from Freud's elucidation of the Oedipus complex in the form of an alleged desire, conscious or unconscious, of male infants to sleep with their mothers. How many young boys do in fact seriously harbour such sexual desires? With respect to Freud, whilst the young clearly need attachment to their mothers, the Oedipal complex as an explanation of human development is no longer regarded with the reverence it once was.

On the other hand we can still point to sons competing with their fathers. That part of the Oedipus story has the truer resonance.

Neville Spencer Lewis,
March 2021

ACKNOWLEDGEMENTS

This book ultimately owes itself to the scholar and topographer Professor Eugene Vanderpool of the American School of Classical Studies in Athens who in addition to other help once drew for me from memory a detailed map of the area of the Phocicon, the meeting place of the Phocians (which he had excavated), and of the Schist Road, and thereby first interested me in the region's history. My fascination with Oedipus had begun much earlier when at school we had performed a Greek play, the Phoenissae, in which in that version of the story the blind Oedipus is driven into exile. His exit was accompanied by part of Sibelius' 5th Symphony, and that was also the beginning of my love of classical music.

I wish then to record my thanks to my proof-reader Adam Haines who made very helpful comments about the content and then prepared the book for publication. Without him it would not have happened.

Neville Spencer Lewis first travelled to Greece as a boy when he fell in love with the country and he went on to read Classics at Oxford University. He later lived in the village of Davlia (ancient Daulis), which is near the Branching Road, affording him a deep knowledge of the area. He is co-writer of the *Guide to Greece* and author of *Delphi and the Sacred Way*, both published by Michael Haag Limited. He lives in London but frequently returns to Greece.

Printed in Great Britain
by Amazon